A scrap of my knitting
work, — with apologies for
the dropped stitches.' —
  Zona Gale
Christmas 1912.-

CHRISTMAS

THE MACMILLAN COMPANY
NEW YORK · BOSTON · CHICAGO
DALLAS · SAN FRANCISCO

MACMILLAN & CO., Limited
LONDON · BOMBAY · CALCUTTA
MELBOURNE

THE MACMILLAN CO. OF CANADA, Ltd.
TORONTO

"MARY FILLED HER ARMS WITH HAY AND TURNED TO THE MANGER"

CHRISTMAS

A STORY

BY

ZONA GALE

AUTHOR OF "THE LOVES OF PELLEAS AND ETARRE"
"FRIENDSHIP VILLAGE," ETC.

WITH ILLUSTRATIONS BY

LEON V. SOLON

New York
THE MACMILLAN COMPANY
1912

All rights reserved

COPYRIGHT, 1912,
BY THE McCLURE PUBLICATIONS, INCORPORATED.

COPYRIGHT, 1912,
BY THE MACMILLAN COMPANY.

Set up and electrotyped. Published October, 1912.

Norwood Press
J. S. Cushing Co. — Berwick & Smith Co.
Norwood, Mass., U.S.A.

ILLUSTRATIONS

"Mary filled her arms with hay, and turned to the manger" . . . . . . *Frontispiece*

                                                          FACING PAGE

"He stood looking at it from part way across the road"   76

"Across the still fields came flashing the point of flame" 110

"The children began to sing, 'Go bury Saint Nicklis'"   150

"Their way led east between high banks of snow" . 200

"The three men stepped into the lamplight" . . 240

CHRISTMAS

I

IT was in October that Mary Chavah burned over the grass of her lawn, and the flame ran free across the place where in Spring her wild flower bed was made. Two weeks later she had there a great patch of purple violets. And all Old Trail Town, which takes account of its neighbours' flowers, of the migratory birds, of eclipses, and the like, came to see the wonder.

"Mary Chavah!" said most of the village, "you're the luckiest woman alive. If a miracle was bound to happen, it'd get itself happened to you."

"I don't believe in miracles, though," Mary wrote to Jenny Wing. "These come just natural — only we don't know how."

"That *is* miracles," Jenny wrote back. "They do come natural — we don't know how."

"At this rate," said Ellen Bourne, one of Mary's neighbours, "you'll be having roses bloom in your yard about Christmas time. For a Christmas present."

"I don't believe in Christmas," Mary said. "I thought you knew that. But I'll take the roses, though, if they come in the Winter," she added, with her queer flash of smile.

When it was dusk, or early in the morning, Mary Chavah, with her long shawl over her head, stooped beside the violets and loosened the earth about them with her whole hand, and as if she reverenced violets more than finger tips. And she thought: —

"Ain't it just as if Spring was right over back of the air all the time — and it could come if we knew how to call it? But we don't know."

But whatever she thought about it, Mary kept in her heart. For it was as if not only Spring, but new life, or some other holy thing were nearer than one thought and had spoken to her, there on the edge of Winter.

And Old Trail Town asked itself:—

"Ain't Mary Chavah the funniest? Look how nice she is about everything — and yet you know she won't never keep Christmas at all. No, sir. She ain't kept a single Christmas in years. I donno why. . . ."

II

Moving about on his little lawn in the dark, Ebenezer Rule was aware of two deeper shadows before him. They were between him and the leafless lilacs and mulberries that lined the street wall. A moment before he had been looking at that darkness and remembering how, once, as a little boy, he had slept there under the wall and had dreamed that he had a kingdom.

"Who is't?" he asked sharply.

"Hello, Ebenezer," said Simeon Buck, "it's only me and Abel. We're all."

Ebenezer Rule came toward them. It was so dark that they could barely distinguish each other. Their voices had to do it all.

"What you doing out here?" one of the deeper shadows demanded.

"Oh, nothing," said Ebenezer, irritably, "not a thing."

He did not ask them to go in the house, and the three stood there awkwardly, handling the time like a blunt instrument. Then Simeon Buck, proprietor of the Simeon Buck North American Dry Goods Exchange, plunged into what they had come to say.

"Ebenezer," he said, with those variations of intonation which mean an effort to be delicate, "is — is there any likelihood that the factory will open up this Fall?"

"No, there ain't," Ebenezer said, like something shutting.

"Nor — nor this Winter?" Simeon pursued.

"No, sir," said Ebenezer, like something opening again to shut with a bang.

"Well, if you're sure —" said Simeon.

Ebenezer cut him short. "I'm dead sure," he said. "I've turned over my orders to my brother's house in the City. He can handle 'em all and not have to pay his men a cent more wages." And this was as if something had been locked.

"Well," said Simeon, "then, Abel, I move we go ahead."

Abel Ames, proprietor of the Granger County Merchandise Emporium ("The A. T. Stewart's of the Middle West," he advertised it), sighed heavily — a vast, triple sigh, that seemed to sigh both in and out, as a schoolboy whistles.

"Well," he said, "I hate to do it. But I'll be billblowed if I want to think of paying for a third or so of this town's Christmas presents and carrying 'em right through the Winter. I done that last year, and Fourth of July I had all I could do to keep from wishing most of the crowd Merry Christmas, 'count of their still owing me. I'm a merchant and a citizen, but I ain't no patent adjustable Christmas tree."

"Me neither," Simeon said. "Last year it was *me* give a silk cloak and a Five Dollar umberella and a fur bore and a bushel of knick-knicks to the folks in this town. My name wa'n't on the cards, but it's me that's paid for 'em — *up* to now. I'm sick of it. The storekeepers of this town may make a good thing out of Christmas, but they'd ought to get some of the credit instead of giving it all, by Josh."

"What you going to do?" inquired Ebenezer, dryly.

"Well, of course last year was an exceptional year," said Abel, "owing —"

He hesitated to say "owing to the failure of the Ebenezer Rule Factory Company," and so stammered with the utmost delicacy, and skipped a measure.

"And we thought," Simeon finished, "that

if the factory wasn't going to open up this Winter, we'd work things so's to have little or no Christmas in town this year — being so much of the present giving falls on us to carry on our books."

"It ain't only the factory wages, of course," Abel interposed, "it's the folks's savings being et up in —"

"— the failure," he would have added, but skipped a mere beat instead.

"— and we want to try to give 'em a chance to pay us up for last Christmas before they come on to themselves with another celebration," he added reasonably.

Ebenezer Rule laughed — a descending scale of laughter that seemed to have no organs wherewith to function in the open, and so never got beyond the gutturals.

"How you going to fix it?" he inquired again.

"Why," said Simeon, "everybody in town's

talking that they ain't going to give anybody anything for Christmas. Some means it and some don't. Some'll do it and some'll back out. But the churches has decided to omit Christmas exercises altogether this year. Some thought to have speaking pieces, but everybody concluded if they had exercises without oranges and candy the children'd go home disappointed, so they've left the whole thing slide —"

"It don't seem just right for 'em not to celebrate the birth of our Lord just because they can't afford the candy," Abel Ames observed mildly, but Simeon hurried on: —

"— slide, and my idea and Abel's is to get the town meeting to vote a petition to the same effect asking the town not to try to do anything with their Christmas this year. We heard the factory wasn't going to open, and we thought if we could tell 'em that for sure, it would settle it — and save him and me and all the rest of 'em. Would — would you be willing for us to tell the town meeting that? It's to-night — we're on the way there."

"Sure," said Ebenezer Rule, "tell 'em. And you might point out to 'em," he added, with his spasm of gutturals, "that failures is often salutary measures. Public benefactions. Fixes folks so's they can't spend their money fool."

He walked with them across the lawn, going between them and guiding them among the empty aster beds.

"They think I et up their savings in the failure," he went on, "when all I done is to bring 'em face to face with the fact that for years they've been overspending themselves. It takes Christmas to show that up. This whole Christmas business is about wore out, anyhow. Ain't it?"

"That's what," Simeon said, "it's a spendin' sham, from edge to edge."

Abel Ames was silent. The three skirted the flower beds and came out on the level sweep of turf before the house that was no house in the darkness, save that they remembered how it looked: a square, smoked thing, with a beard of dead creepers and white shades lidded over its never-lighted windows — a fit home for this man least-liked of the three hundred neighbours who made Old Trail Town. He touched the elbows of the other two men as they walked in the dark, but he rarely touched any human being. And now Abel Ames suddenly put his hand down on that of Ebenezer, where it lay in the crook of Abel's elbow.

"What you got there?" he asked.

"Nothing much," Ebenezer answered, irritably again. "It's an old glass. I was looking over some rubbish, and I found it — over back. It's a field glass."

"What you got a field glass out in the dark for?" Abel demanded.

"I used to fool with it some when I was a little shaver," Ebenezer said. He put the glass in Abel's hand. "On the sky," he added.

Abel lifted the glass and turned it on the heavens. There, above the little side lawn, the firmament had unclothed itself of branches and lay in a glorious nakedness to three horizons.

"Thunder," Abel said, "look at 'em look."

Sweeping the field with the lens, Abel spoke meanwhile.

"Seems as if I'd kind of miss all the fuss in the store around Christmas," he said,—"the extra rush and the trimming up and all."

"Abel'll miss lavishin' his store with cut paper, I guess," said Simeon; "he dotes on tassels."

"Last year," Abel went on, not lowering the glass, "I had a little kid come in the store

CHRISTMAS 13

Christmas Eve, that I'd never see before. He ask' me if he could get warm — and he set down on the edge of a chair by the stove, and he took in everything in the place. I ask' him his name, and he just smiled. I ask' him if he was glad it was Christmas, and he says, Was I. I was goin' to give him some cough drops, but when I come back from waiting on somebody he was gone. I never could find out who he was, nor see anybody that saw him. I thought mebbe this Christmas he'd come back. Lord, don't it look like a pasture of buttercups up there? Here, Simeon."

Simeon, talking, took the glass and lifted it to the stars.

"Cut paper doin's is all very well," he said, "but the worst nightmare of the year to the stores is Christmas. I always think it's come to be 'Peace on earth, good will to men and extravagance of women.' Quite a nice little till of gold pieces up there in the sky, ain't there? I'd kind o' like to stake a claim out up there — eh? Lay it out along about around that bright one down there — by Josh," he broke off, "look at that bright one."

Simeon kept looking through the glass, and he leaned a little forward to try to see the better.

"What is it?" he repeated, "what's that one? It's the biggest star I ever see —"

The other two looked where he was looking, low in the east. But they saw nothing save boughs indeterminately moving and a spatter of sparkling points not more bright than those of the upper field.

"You look," Simeon bade the vague presence that was his host; but through the glass, Ebenezer still saw nothing that challenged his sight.

"I don't know the name of a star in the sky,

except the dipper," he grumbled, "but I don't see anything out of the ordinary, anyhow."

"It is," Simeon protested; "I tell you, it's the biggest star I ever saw. It's blue and purple and green and yellow —"

Abel had the glass now, and he had looked hardly sooner than he had recognized.

"Sure," he said, "I've got it. It *is* blue and purple and green and yellow, and it's as big as most stars put together. It twinkles — yes, sir, and it swings . . . " he broke off, laughing at the mystification of the others, and laughed so that he could not go on.

"Is it a comet, do you s'pose?" said Simeon.

"No," said Abel, "no. It's come to stay. It's our individual private star. It's the arc light in front of the Town Hall you two are looking at."

They moved to where Abel stood, and from there, up the rise of ground to the east, they could see Simeon's star, shining softly and throwing long rays, it seemed, almost to where they stood: the lamp that marked the heart of the village.

"Shucks," said Simeon.

"Sold," said Ebenezer.

"Why, I don't know," said Abel, "I kind of like to see it through the glass. It looks like it was a bigger light than we give it credit for."

"It's a big enough light," said Ebenezer, testily. It was his own plant at the factory that made possible the town's three arc lights, and these had been continued by him at the factory's closing.

"No use making fun of your friends' eyesight because you're all of twenty minutes younger than them," Simeon grumbled. "Come on, Abel. It must be gettin' round the clock."

Abel lingered.

"A man owns the hull thing with a glass o'

this stamp," he said. "How much does one like that cost?" he inquired.

"I'll sell you this one —" began Ebenezer; "wait a week or two and I may sell you this one," he said. "I ain't really looked through it myself yet."

Not much after this, the two went away and left Ebenezer in the dark yard.

He stood in the middle of his little grass plot and looked through his glass again. That night there was, so to say, nothing remote about the sky, save its distance. It had none of the reticence of clouds. It made you think of a bed of golden bells, each invisible stalk trying on its own account to help forward some Spring. As he had said, he did not know one star from another, nor a planet for a planet with a name. It had been years since he had seen the heavens so near. He moved about, looking, and passed the wall of leafless lilacs and mulberries.

Stars hung in his boughs like fruit for the plucking. They patterned patches of sky. He looked away and back, and it was as if the stars repeated themselves, like the chorus of everything.

"You beggars," Ebenezer said, "awful dressed up, ain't you? It must be for something up there — it ain't for anything down here, let me tell you."

He went up to his dark back door. From without there he could hear Kate Kerr, his general servant, who had sufficient personality to compel the term "housekeeper," setting sponge for bread, with a slapping, hollow sound and a force that implied a frown for every down stroke of the iron spoon. He knew how she would turn toward the door as he entered, with her way of arching eyebrows, in the manner of one about to recite the symptoms of a change for the worse — or at best to say "about the same" to everything in the universe. And

CHRISTMAS 19

when Kate Kerr spoke, she always whispered on the faintest provocation.

A sudden distaste for the entire inside of his house seized Ebenezer. He turned and wandered back down the little dark yard, looking up at the high field of the stars, with only his dim eyes.

"There must be quite a little to know about them," he thought, "if anybody was enough inter-ested."

Then he remembered Simeon and Abel, and laughed again in his way.

"I done the town a good turn for once, didn't I?" he thought; "I've fixed folks so's they can't spend their money fool!"

Two steps from Ebenezer's front gate, Simeon and Abel overtook a woman. She had a long shawl over her head, and she was humming some faint air of her own making.

"Coming to the meeting, Mary?" Simeon asked as they passed her.

"No," said Mary Chavah, "I started for it. But it's such a nice night I'm going to walk around."

"Things are going to go your way to that meeting, I guess," said Simeon; "ain't you always found fault with Christmas?"

"They's a lot o' nonsense about it," Mary assented; "I don't ever bother myself much with it. Why?"

"I donno but we'll all come round to your way of thinking to-night," said Simeon.

"For just this year!" Abel Ames called back, as they went on.

"You can't do much else, I guess," said Mary. "Everybody dips Christmas up out of their pocketbooks, and if there ain't nothing there, they can't dip."

The men laughed with her, and went on down the long street toward the town. Mary followed slowly, under the yellowing elms that made great golden shades for the dim post lamps. And high at the far end of the street down which they went, hung the blue arc light before the Town Hall, center to the constellation of the home lights and the shop lights and the street lights, all near neighbours to the stream and sweep of the stars hanging a little higher and shining as by one sun.

III

It was interesting to see how they took the proposal to drop that Christmas from the calendar there in Old Trail Town. It was so eminently a sensible thing to do, and they all knew it. Oh, every way they looked at it, it was sensible, and they admitted it. Yet, besides Mary Chavah and Ebenezer Rule, probably the only person in the town whose satisfaction in the project could be counted on to be unfeigned was little Tab Winslow. For Tab, as all the town knew, had a turkey brought up by his own hand to be the Winslows' Christmas dinner, but such had become Tab's intimacy with and fondness for the turkey that he was prepared to forego his Christmas if only that dinner were foregone, too.

"Theophilus Thistledown is such a human turkey," Tab had been heard explaining patiently; "he knows me — and he knows his name. He don't *expect* us to eat him . . . why, you *can't* eat anything that knows its name."

But every one else was just merely sensible. And they had been discussing Christmas in this sensible strain at the town meeting that night, before Simeon and Abel broached their plan for standardizing their sensible leanings.

Somebody had said that Jenny Wing, and Bruce Rule, who was Ebenezer's nephew, were expected home for Christmas, and had added that it "didn't look as if there would be much of any Christmas down to the station to meet them." On which Mis' Mortimer Bates had spoken out, philosophical to the point of brutality. Mis' Bates was little and brown and quick, and her clothes seemed always to curtain her off, so that her figure was no part of her presence.

"I ain't going to do a thing for Christmas this year," she declared, as nearly everybody in the village had intermittently declared, "not a living, breathing thing. I can't, and folks might just as well know it, flat foot. What's the use of buying tinsel and flim-flam when you're eating milk gravy to save butter and using salt sacks for handkerchiefs? I ain't educated up to see it."

Mis' Jane Moran, who had changed her chair three times to avoid a draught, sat down carefully in her fourth chair, her face twitching a little as if its muscles were connected with her joints.

"Christmas won't be no different from any other day to our house this year," she said. "We'll get up and eat our three meals and sit down and look at each other. We can't even spare a hen — she might lay if we didn't eat her."

Mis' Abby Winslow, mother of seven under fifteen, looked up from her rocking-chair — Mis' Winslow always sat limp in chairs as if they were reaching out to rest her and, indeed, this occasional yielding to the force of gravity was almost her only luxury.

"You ain't thinking of the children, Mis' Bates," she said, "nor you either, Jane Moran, or you couldn't talk that way. We can't have no real Christmas, of course. But I'd planned some little things made out of what I had in the house: things that wouldn't be anything, and yet would seem a little something."

Mis' Mortimer Bates swept round at her.

"Children," she said, "ought to be showed how to do without things. Bennet and Gussie ain't expecting a sliver of nothing for Christmas — not a sliver."

Mis' Winslow unexpectedly flared up.

"Whether it shows through on the outside or not," she said, "I'll bet you they are."

"My three," Mis' Emerson Morse put in pacifically, "have been kept from popping corn and cracking nuts all Fall so's they could do both Christmas night, and it would seem like something that *was* something."

"That ain't the idea," Mis' Bates insisted; "I want them learnt to do without —" ("They'll learn that," Mis' Abby Winslow said; "they'll learn . . .") "Happening as it does to most every one of us not to have no Christmas, they won't be no distinctions drawn. None of the children can brag — and children is limbs of Satan for bragging," she added. (She was remembering a brief conversation overheard that day between Gussie and Pep, the minister's son: —

"I've got a doll," said Gussie.

"I've got a dollar," said Pep.

"My mamma went to a tea party," said Gussie.

"My mamma give one," said Pep.

Gussie mustered her forces. "My papa goes to work every morning," she topped it.

"My papa don't have to," said Pep, and closed the incident.)

"I can't help who's a limb of Satan," Mis' Winslow replied doggedly, "I can't seem to sense Christmas time without Christmas."

"It won't *be* Christmas time if you don't have any Christmas," Mis' Bates persisted.

"Oh, yes it will," Mis' Winslow said. "Oh, yes, it will. You can't stop that."

It was Mis' Bates, who, from the high-backed plush rocker, rapped with the blue glass paperweight on the red glass lamp and, in the absence of Mr. Bates, called the meeting to order. The Old Trail Town Society was organized on a platform of "membership unlimited, dues nothing but taking turns with the entertaining, officers to consist of: President, the host of the evening (or wife, if any), and no minutes to bother with." And it was to a meeting so disposed on the subject of Christmas that Simeon Buck rose to present his argument.

"Mr. President," he addressed the chair.

"It's Madam President, you ninny geese," corrected Buff Miles, *sotto voce*.

"It had ought to be Madam Chairman," objected Mis' Moran; "she ain't the continuous president."

"Well, for the land sakes, call me Mis' Bates, formal, and go ahead," said the lady under discussion. "Only I bet you've forgot now what you was going to say."

"Not much I did *not*," Simeon Buck continued composedly, and, ignoring the interruptions, let his own vocative stand. Then he presented a memorandum of a sum of money. It was not a large sum. But when he quoted it, everybody looked at everybody else, stricken. For it was a sum large enough to have required, in the earning, months of work on the part of an appalling proportion of Old Trail Town.

"From the day after Thanksgiving to the night before Christmas last year," said Simeon, "that is the amount that the three hundred souls — no, I guess it must have been bodies — in our town spent in the local stores. Now, bare living expenses aside, — which ain't very much for us all, these days, — this amount may be assumed to have been spent by the lot of us for Christmas. Of course there was those," continued Mr. Buck, looking intelligently about him, "who bought most of their Christmas stuff in the City. But these — these economic traitors only make the point of what I say the more so. Without them, the town spent this truly amazing sum in keeping the holidays. Now, I ask you, frank, could the town afford that, or anything like that?"

Buff Miles spoke out of the extremity of his reflections.

"That's a funny crack," he said, "for a merchant to make. Why not leave 'em spend and leave 'em pay?"

"Oh, I'll leave 'em *pay* all right," rejoined Simeon, significantly, and stood silent and smiling until there were those in the room who uncomfortably shifted.

Then he told them the word he bore from Ebenezer Rule that as they had feared and half expected, the factory was not to open that Winter at all. Hardly a family represented in the rooms was not also representative of a factory employee, now idle these seven months, as they were periodically idle at the times of "enforced" suspension of the work.

"What I'm getting at is this," Simeon summed it up, "and Abel Ames, here, backs me up—don't you, Abel?—that hadn't we all ought to come to some joint conclusion about our Christmas this year, and roust the town up to it, like a town, and not go it blind and either get in up to our necks in debt, same as City folks, or else quit off Christmas, individual, and mebbe hurt folks's feelings? Why not move intelligent, like a town, and all agree out-and-out to leave Christmas go by this year? And have it understood, thorough?"

It was very still in the little rooms when he had finished. There seems to be no established etiquette of revolutions. But something of the unconsciousness of the enthusiast was upon Mis' Mortimer Bates, and she spoke before she knew:—

"So's we can be sure everybody else'll know it and not give something either and be disappointed too," she assented. "Well, I bet everybody'd be real relieved."

"The churches has sanctioned us doing away with Christmas this year by doing away with it themselves," observed Mis' Jane Moran. "That'd ought to be enough to go by."

"It don't seem to me Christmas is a thing for the churches to decide about," said Simeon, thoughtfully. "It seems to me the matter is up to the merchants and the grocers and the family providers. We're the ones most concerned. Us providers have got to scratch gravel to get together any Christmas at all, if any. And speaking for us merchants, I may say, we'll lay in the stock if folks'll buy it. But if they can't afford to pay for it, we don't want the stock personally."

"I guess we've all had the experience," observed Mis' Jane Moran, "of announcing we wasn't going to give any gifts *this* year, and then had somebody send something embroidered by hand, with a solid month's work on it. But if we all agree to secede from Christmas, we can lay down the law to folks so's it'll be understood: *No Christmas for nobody.*"

"Not to children?" said Mis' Abby Winslow, doubtfully.

"My idea is to teach 'em to do entirely without Christmas," harped Mis' Bates. "We can't afford one. Why not let the children share in the family privation without trying to fool 'em with make-shift presents and boiled sugar?"

Over in a corner near the window plants, whose dead leaves she had been picking off, sat Ellen Bourne — Mis' Matthew Bourne she was, but nearly everybody called her Ellen Bourne. There is some law about these things: why instinctively we call some folk by the whole name, some by their first names, some by the last, some by shortening the name, some by a name not their own. Perhaps there is a name for each of us, if only we knew where to look, and folk intuitively select the one most like that. Perhaps some of us, by the sort of miracle that is growing every day, got the name that is meant for us. Perhaps some of us struggle along with consonants that spell somebody else. And how did some names get themselves so terrifically overused unless by some strange might, say, a kind of astrological irregularity . . . Ellen Bourne sat by the window and suddenly looked over her shoulder at the room.

"If we've got the things made," she said, "can't we give 'em? If it's to children?"

"I think if we're going to omit, we'd ought to omit," Mis Bates held her own; "it can't matter to you, Ellen, with no children, so . . ."

She caught herself sharply up. Ellen's little boy had died a Christmas or two ago.

"No," Ellen said, "I ain't any children, of course. But —"

"Well, I think," said Mis' Jane Moran, "that we've hit on the only way we could have hit on to chirk each other up over a hard time."

"And get off delicate ourselves same time," said Buff Miles. From the first Buff had been advocating what he called "an open Christmas," and there were those near him at the meeting to whom he had confided some plan about "church choir Christmas carol serenades," which he was loath to see set at naught.

Not much afterward Simeon Buck put the motion: —

"Mis' Chairman," he said, "I move you — and all of us — that the Old Trail Town meeting do and hereby does declare itself in favour of striking Christmas celebrations from its calendar this year. And that we circulate a petition through the town to this effect, headed by our names. And that we all own up that it's for the simple and regretful reason that not a mother's son of us can afford to buy Christmas presents this year, and what's the use of scratching to keep up appearances?"

For a breath Abel Ames hesitated; then he spoke voluntarily for the first time that evening.

"Mr. President, I second the hull of that," said he, slowly, and without looking at anybody; and then sighed his vast, triple sigh.

There was apparently nobody to vote against the motion. Mis' Winslow did not vote at all. Ellen Bourne said "No," but she said it so faintly that nobody heard save those nearest her, and they felt a bit embarrassed for her because she had spoken alone, and they tried to cover up the minute.

"Carried," said the Chair, and slipped out in the kitchen to put on the coffee.

At the meeting there was almost nobody who, in the course of the evening, did not make or reply to some form of observation on one theme. It was:—

"Well, I wish Mary Chavah'd been to the meeting. She'd have enjoyed herself."

Or, "Well, won't Mary Chavah be glad of this plan they've got? She's wanted it a good while."

Or, "We all seem to have come to Mary Chavah's way of thinking, don't we? You know, she ain't kept any Christmas for years."

Unless it was Abel Ames. He, in fact, made or replied to almost no observations that evening. He drank his coffee without cream, sugar, or spoon,—they are always overlooking somebody's essentials in this way, and such is Old Trail Town's shy courtesy that the omission is never mentioned or repaired by the victim, — and sighed his triple sigh at intervals, and went home.

"Hetty," he said to his wife, who had not gone to the meeting, "they put it through. We won't have no Christmas creditors this year. We don't have to furnish charged Christmas presents for nobody."

She looked up from the towel she was featherstitching — she was a little woman who carried her head back and had large eyes and the long, curved lashes of a child.

"I s'pose you're real relieved, ain't you, Abel?" she answered.

"My, yes," said Abel, without expression. "My, yes."

They all took the news home in different wise.

"Matthew," said Ellen Bourne, "the town meeting voted not to have any Christmas this year. That is, to ask the folks not to have any — 'count of expense."

"Sensible move," said Matthew, sharpening his ax by the kitchen stove.

"It'll be a relief for most folks not to have the muss and the clutter," said Ellen's mother.

"Hey, king and country!" said Ellen's old father, whittling a stick, "I ain't done no more'n look on at a Christmas for ten years and more — with no children around so."

"I know," said Ellen Bourne, "I know. . . ."

The announcement was greeted by Mortimer Bates with a slap of the knee.

"Good-by, folderol!" he said. "We need a sane Christmas in the world a good sight more'n we need a sane Fourth, most places. Good work."

But Bennet and Gussie Bates burst into wails.

"Hush!" said Mis' Bates, peremptorily.

"You ain't the only ones, remember. It's no Christmas for nobody!"

"I thought the rest of 'em would have one an' we could go over to theirs . . ." sobbed Gussie.

"I'd rather p'etend it's Christmas in other houses even if we ain't it!" mourned Bennet.

"Be my little man and woman," admonished Mis' Mortimer Bates.

At the Morans, little Emily Moran made an unexpected deduction: —

"I *won't* stay in bed all day Christmas!" she gave out.

"Stay in bed!" echoed Mis' Moran. "Why on this earth should you stay in bed?"

"Well, if we get up, then it's Christmas and you can't stop it!" little Emily triumphed.

When they told Pep, the minister's son, after a long preparation by story and other gradual approach, and a Socratic questioning cleverly winning damning admissions from Pep, he looked up in his father's face thoughtfully: —

"If they ain't no Christ's birthday this year, is it a lie that Christ was born?" he demanded.

And secretly the children took counsel with one another: Would Buff Miles, the church choir tenor, take them out after dark on Christmas Eve, to sing church choir serenades at folks' gates, or would he not? And when they thought that he might not, because this would be considered Christmas celebration and would only make the absence of present-giving the more conspicuous, as in the case of the Sunday schools themselves, they faced still another theological quandary: For if it was true that Christ was born, then Christmas was his birthday; and if Christmas was his birthday, wasn't it wicked not to pay any attention?

Alone of them all, little Tab Winslow rejoiced. His brothers and sisters made the time tearful with questionings as to the effect on Santa Claus, and how would they get word to him, and would it be Christmas in the City, and why couldn't they move there, and other matters denoting the reversal of this their earth. But Tab slipped out the kitchen door, to the corner of the barn, where the great turkey gobbler who had been named held his empire trustingly.

"Oh, Theophilus Thistledown," said Tab to him, "you're the only one in this town that's goin' to have a Christmas. You ain't got to be et."

IV

The placard was tacked to the Old Trail Town post-office wall, between a summons to join the Army and the Navy of the United States, and the reward offered for an escaped convict — all three manifestoes registering something of the stage of society's development.

NOTICE

Owing to the local business depression and to the current private decisions to get up very few home Christmas celebrations this year, and also to the vote of the various lodges, churches, Sunday schools, etc., etc., etc., to forego the usual Christmas tree observances, the merchants of this town have one and all united with most of the folks to petition the rest to omit all Christmas presents, believing that the Christmas spirit will be kept up best by all agreeing to act alike. All that's willing may announce it by signing below and notifying others.

THE COMMITTEE.

There were only three hundred folk living in Old Trail Town. Already two thirds of their signatures were scrawled on the sheets of foolscap tacked beneath the notice.

On the day after her return home, Jenny Wing stood and stared at the notice. Her mother had written to her of the town's talk, but the placard made it seem worse.

"I'll go in on the way home and see what Mary says," she thought, and asked for the letter that lay in Mary Chavah's box, next her own. They gave her the letter without question. All Old Trail Town asks for its neighbour's mail and reads its neighbour's postmarks and gets to know the different Writings and to

CHRISTMAS 45

inquire after them, like persons. ("He ain't got so much of a curl to his M to-day," one will say of a superscription. "Better write right back and chirk 'im up." Or, "Here's Her that don't seal her letters good. Tell her about that, why don't you?" Or, "This Writing's a stranger to me. I'll just wait a minute to see if birth or death gets out of the envelope.")

As she closed Mary's gate and hurried up the walk, in a keen wind flowing with little pricking flakes, Jenny was startled to see both parlour windows open. The white muslin curtains were blowing idly as if June were in the air. Turning as a matter of course to the path that led to the kitchen, she was hailed by Mary, who came out the front door with a rug in her hands.

"Step right in this way," said Mary; "this door's unfastened."

"Forevermore!" Jenny said, "Mary Chavah! What you got your house all open for? You ain't moving?"

A gust of wind took Mary's answer. She tossed the rug across the icy railing of the porch and beckoned Jenny into the house, and into the parlour. And when she had greeted Jenny after the months of her absence:—

"See," Mary said exultantly, "don't it look grand and empty? Look at it first, and then come on in and I'll tell you about it."

The white-papered walls of the two rooms were bare of pictures; the floor had been sparingly laid with rugs. The walnut sofa and chairs, the table for the lamp, and the long shelves of her grandfather's books — these were all that the room held. A white arch divided the two chambers, like a benign brow whose face had long been dimmed away. It was all exquisitely clean and icy cold. A little snow drifted in through the muslin curtains. The breath of the two women showed.

"What on earth you done that for?" Jenny demanded.

Mary Chavah stood in the empty archway, the satisfaction on her face not veiling its pure austerity. She was not much past thirty-three, but she looked older, for she was gaunt. Her flesh had lost its firmness, her dressmaking had stooped her, her strong frame moved as if it habitually shouldered its way. In her broad forehead and deep eyes and somewhat in her silent mouth, you read the woman — the rest of her was obscured in her gentle reticence. She had a gray shawl, blue-bordered, folded tightly about her head and pinned under her chin, and it wrapped her to her feet.

"I feel like a thing in a new shell," she said. "Come on in where it's warm."

Instead of moving her dining-room table to her kitchen, as most of Old Trail Town did in Winter, Mary had moved her cooking stove into the dining room, had improvised a calico-curtained cupboard for the utensils, and there she lived and sewed. The windows were bare.

"I'll let the parlour have curtains if it wants to," she had said, "but in the room I live in I want every strip of the sun I can get."

There were no plants, though every house in Old Trail Town had a window of green, and slips without number were offered. . . .

" . . . You can have flowers all you want," she said once; "I like 'em too well to box 'em up in the house."

And there were no books.

"I don't read," she admitted; "I ain't ever read a book in my life but "Pilgrim's Progress" and the first four chapters of "Ben Hur." What's the use of pretending, when books is such a nuisance to dust? Grandfather's books in the parlour — oh, they ain't books. They're furniture."

But she had a little bookcase whose shelves were filled with her patterns — in her dressmaking she never used a fashion plate.

"I like to make 'em up and cut 'em out," she sometimes told her friends. "I don't care nothing whatever about the dresses when they get done — more fool the women for ornamenting themselves up like lamp shades, I always think. But I just do love to fuss with the paper and make it do like I say. Land, I've got my cupboard full of more patterns than I'd ever get orders for if I lived to be born again."

She sat down before the cooking stove and drew off her woolen mittens. She folded a hand on her cheek, forcing the cheek out of drawing by her hand's pressure. There was always about her gestures a curious nakedness — indeed, about her face and hands. They were naïve, perfectly likely to reveal themselves in their current awkwardness and ugliness of momentary expression which, by its very frankness, made a new law as it broke an old one.

"Don't you tell folks I've been house cleaning," she warned Jenny. "The town would think I was crazy, with the thermometer acting up zero so. Anyway, I ain't been house cleaning. I just simply got so sick to death of all the truck piled up in this house that I had to get away from it. And this morning it looked so clean and white and smooth outdoors that I felt so cluttered up I couldn't sew. I begun on this room — and then I kept on with the parlour. I've took out the lambrequins and 'leven pictures and the what-not and four moth-catching rugs and four sofa pillows, and I've packed the whole lot of 'em into the attic. I've done the same to my bedroom. I've emptied my house out of all the stuff the folks' and the folks' folks and their folks — clear back to Grandmother Hackett had in here — I mean the truck part. Not the good. And I guess now I've got some room to live in."

Jenny looked at her admiringly, and asked: "How did you ever do it? I can't bear to throw things away. I can't bear to move things from where they've been."

"I didn't use to want to," said Mary, "but lately — I do. The Winter's so clean, you kind of have to, to keep up. What's the news?"

"Here's a letter," Jenny said, and handed it. "I didn't look to see who it's from. I guess it's a strange Writing, anyway."

Mary glanced indifferently at it. "It's from Lily's boy, out West," she said, and laid the letter on the shelf. "I meant, what's the news about you?"

Jenny's eyes widened swiftly. "News about me?" she said. "Who said there was any news about me?"

"Nobody," Mary said evenly; "but you've been gone most a year, ain't you?"

"Oh," Jenny said, "yes . . ."

For really, when Old Trail Town stopped to think of it, Jenny Wing was Mrs. Bruce Rule, and had been so for a year. But no one thought of calling her that. It always takes Old Trail Town several years to adopt its marriages. They would graduate first to "Jenny Wing that was," and then to "Jenny Wing What's-name," and then to "Mis' Rule that was Jenny Wing. . . ."

". . . You tell me some news," Jenny added. "Mother don't ever write much but the necessaries."

"That's all there's been," Mary Chavah told her; "we ain't had no luxuries for news in forever."

"But there's that notice in the post office," cried Jenny. "I come home to spend Christmas, and there's that notice in the post office. Mother wrote nobody was going to do anything for Christmas, but she never wrote me that. I've brought home some little things I made —"

"Oh — Christmas!" Mary said. "Yes, they all got together and concluded best not have any. You know, since the failure —"

Mary hesitated — Ebenezer Rule was Bruce Rule's uncle.

"I know," said Jenny, "it's Uncle Ebenezer. I don't know how I'm going to tell Bruce when he comes. To think it's in our family, the reason they can't have any Christmas. . . ."

"Nonsense," said Mary, briskly; "no Christmas presents is real sensible, my way of thinking. It's been 'leven years since I've given a Christmas present to anybody. The first Christmas after mother died, I couldn't — I just couldn't. That kind of got me out of the i-dea, and then I see all the nonsense of it."

"The *nonsense?*" Jenny repeated.

"If you don't like folks, you don't want to give nothing to them or take nothing from them. And if you do like 'em you don't want to have to wait to Christmas to give 'em things. Ain't that so?" Mary Chavah put it.

"*No*," said Jenny, "it ain't. Not a bit so." And when Mary laughed, questioned her, pressed her, "It seems perfectly awful to me not to have a Christmas," Jenny could say only, "I feel like the Winter didn't have no backbone to it."

"It's a dead time, Winter," Mary assented. "What's the use of tricking it up with gewgaws and pretending it's a live time? Besides, if you ain't got the money, you ain't got the money. And nobody has, this year. Unless they go ahead and buy things anyway, like the City."

Jenny shook her head. "I got seven Christmas-present relatives and ten Christmas-present friends, and I've only spent Two Dollars and Eighty cents on 'em all," she said, "for material. But I've made little things for every one of 'em. It don't seem as if that much had ought to hurt any one.

Jenny looked past her out the window, somewhere beyond the snow.

"They's something else," she added, "it ain't all present giving. . . ."

"Nonsense," said Mary Chavah, "take the present trading away from Christmas and see how long it'd last. I was in the City once for Christmas. I'll never forget it — never.

I never see folks work like the folks worked there. The streets was Bedlam. The stores was worse. 'What'll I get him? . . .' 'I've just got to get something for her. . . .' 'It don't seem as if this is nice enough after what she give me last year. . . .' I can hear 'em yet. They spent money wicked. And I said to myself that I was glad from my head to my feet that I was done with Christmas. And I been preaching it ever since. And I'm pleased this town has had to come to it."

"It ain't the way I feel," said Jenny. She got up and wandered to the window and hardly heard while Mary went on with more of the sort. "It seems kind of like going back on the ways things are," Jenny said, as she turned. Then, as she made ready to go, she broke off and smote her hands together.

"Oh," she said, "it don't seem as if I could bear it not to have Christmas — not *this* year."

"You mean your and Bruce's first Christmas," said Mary. "Mark my words, he'll be glad to be rid of the fuss. Men always are. Come on out the front door if you're going," said Mary. "You might as well use it when it's open."

As Jenny passed the open parlour door, she looked in again at the bare room.

"Don't you *like* pictures?" she asked abruptly.

"I like 'em when I like 'em," Mary answered. "I didn't like them I had up here — I had a shot stag and a fruit piece and an eagle with a child in its claws. I've loathed 'em for years, but I ain't ever had the heart to throw 'em out till now. They're over behind the coal bin."

Jenny thought. "They's a picture over to mother's," she said, "that she ain't put up because she ain't had the money to frame it. I guess I'll bring it over after supper and see if

you don't want it up here — frame or no frame."
She looked at Mary and laughed. "If I bring
it to you to-night," she said, "it ain't a Christmas present — legal. But if I want to call it
a Christmas present inside me, the town can't
help that."

"What's the picture?" Mary asked.

"I don't know who it represents," said Jenny,
"but it's nice."

When Jenny had gone, Mary Chavah stood
in the snow shaking the rug she had left outside, and looking at the clean, white town.

"It looks like it was waiting for something,"
she thought.

A door opened and shut. A child shouted.
In the north east a shining body had come
sparkling above the trees — Capella of the
brightness of one hundred of our suns, being
born into the twilight like a little star. . . .

Mary closed the parlour windows and stood

for a moment immersed in the quiet and emptiness of the clean rooms.

"This looks like it was waiting for something, too," she thought. "But it ought to know it won't get it," she added whimsically.

Then she went back to the warm room and saw the letter on the shelf. She meant to go in a moment to the stable to make it safe there for the night; so, with the gray shawl still binding her head and falling to her feet, she sat by the stove and read the letter.

V

". . . because she wasn't sick but two days and we never thought of her dying till she was dead. Otherwise we'd have telegraphed. She was buried yesterday, right here, and we'll get some kind of stone. You say how you think it'd ought to be marked. That's about all there is to tell except about *Yes*. He's six years old now and Aunt Mary this ain't a place for him. He's a nice little fellow and I hate for him to get rough and he will if he stays here. I'll do the best I can and earn money to help keep him but I want he should come and live with you. . . ."

"I won't have him!" said Mary Chavah, aloud.

". . . he could come alone with a tag all right and I could send his things by freight. He ain't got much. You couldn't help but like him and I hate for him to get rough. Please answer and oblige your loving Nephew,

"JOHN BLOOD."

Mary kept reading the letter and staring out into the snow. Her sister Lily's boy — they wanted to send him to her. Lily's boy and Adam Blood's — the man whose son she had thought would be her son. It was twenty years ago that he had been coming to the house — this same house — and she had thought that he was coming to see her, had never thought of Lily at all till Lily had told her of her own betrothal to him. It hurt yet. It had hurt freshly when he had died, seven years ago. Now Lily was dead, and Adam's eldest son, John, wanted to send this little brother to her, to have.

"I won't take him," she said a great many times, and kept reading the letter and staring out into the snow.

For Lily she had no tears — she seldom had tears at all. But after a little while she was conscious of a weight through her and in her,

aching in her throat, her breast, her body.
She rose and went near to the warmth of the
fire, then to the freedom of the window against
which the snow lay piled, then she sat down in
the place where she worked, beside her patterns.
The gray shawl still bound her head, and it was
still in her mind that she must go to the barn
and lock it. But she did not go — she sat in
the darkening room with all her past crowding
it. . . .

. . . That first day with Adam at the Blood's
picnic, given at his home-coming. They had
met with all that perilous, ready-made intimacy
which a school friendship of years before had
allowed. As she had walked beside him she
had known well what he was going to mean to
her. She remembered the moment when he
had contrived to ask her to wait until the others
went, so that he might walk home with her.
And when they had reached home, there on

the porch — where she had just shaken the rugs in the snow — Lily had been sitting, a stool — one of the stools now at length banished to the shed — holding the hurt ankle that had kept her from the picnic. Adam had stayed an hour, and they had sat beside Lily. He had come again and again, and they had always sat beside Lily. Mary remembered that those were the days when she was happy in *things* — in the house and the look of the rooms and of the little garden from the porch, and of the old red-cushioned rocking-chairs on the tiny "stoop." She had loved her clothes and her little routines, and all these things had seemed desirable and ultimate because they two were sharing them. Then one day Mary had joined Lily and Adam there on the porch, and Lily had been looking up with new eyes, and Mary had searched her face, and then Adam's face; and they had all seemed in a sudden nakedness; and Mary had known that a great place was closed against her.

Since then house and porch and garden and routines had become like those of other places. She had always been shut outside something, and always she had borne burdens. The death of her parents, gadflys of need, worst of all a curious feeling that the place closed against her was somehow herself — that, so to say, she and herself had never once met. She used to say that to herself sometimes, "There's two of me, and we don't meet — we don't meet."

"And now he wants me to take her boy and Adam's," she kept saying; "I'll never do such a thing — never."

She thought that the news of Lily's death was what gave her the strange, bodily hurt that had seized her — the news that what she was used to was gone; that she had no sister;

CHRISTMAS

that the days of their being together and all the tasks of their upbringing were finished. Then she thought that the remembering of those days of her happiness and her pain, and the ache of what might have been and of what never was, had come to torture her again. But the feeling was rather the weight of some imminent thing, the ravage of something that grew with what it fed on, the grasp upon her of something that would not let her go. . . .

She had never seen them after their marriage, and so she had never seen either of the children. Lily had once sent her a picture of John, but she had never sent one of this other little boy. Mary tried to recall what they had ever said of him. She could not even remember his baptismal name, but she knew that they had called him "Yes" because it was the first word he had learned to say, and because he had said it to everything. "The baby can say 'Yes,'" Lily had written once; "I guess it's all he'll ever be able to say. He says it all day long. He won't try to say anything else." And once later: "We've taken to calling the baby 'Yes,' and now he calls himself that. 'Yes wants it,' he says, and 'Take Yes,' and 'Yes is going off now.' His father likes it. He says yes is everything and no is nothing. I don't think that means much, but we call him that for fun. . . ." But Mary could not remember what the child's real name was. What difference did it make? As if she could have a child meddling round the house while she was sewing. But of course this was not the real reason. The real reason was that she could not bring up a child — did she not know that?

". . . He's six years old now and Aunt Mary this ain't a place for him. He's a nice little fellow and I hate for him to get rough and he will if he stays here. . . ."

She tried to think who else could take him. They had no one. Adam, she knew, had no one. Some of the neighbours there by the ranch . . . it was absurd to send him that long journey . . . so she went through it all, denying with all the old denials. And all the while the weight in her body grew and filled her, and she was strangely conscious of her breath.

"What ails me?" she said aloud, and got up to kindle a light. She was amazed to see that it was seven o'clock, and long past her supper hour. As she took from the clock shelf the key to the barn, some one rapped at the back door and came through the cold kitchen with friendly familiarity. It was Jenny, a shawl over her head, her face glowing with the cold, and in her mittened hands a flat parcel.

"My hand's most froze," Jenny admitted. "I didn't want to roll this thing, so I carried it flat out, and it blew consider'ble. It's the picture."

"Get yourself warm," Mary bade her. "I'll undo it. Who is it of?" she added, as the papers came away.

"That's what I don't know," said Jenny, "but I've always liked it around. I thought maybe you'd know."

It was a picture which, in those days, had not before come to Old Trail Town. The figure was that of a youth, done by a master of the times — the head and shoulders of a youth who seemed to be looking passionately at something outside the picture.

"There it is, anyhow," Jenny added. "If you like it enough to hang it up, hang it up. It's a Christmas present!" Jenny laughed elfishly.

Mary Chavah held the picture out before her.

"I do," she said; "I could take a real fancy

CHRISTMAS 69

to it. I'll have it up on the wall. Much obliged, I'm sure. Set down a minute."

But Jenny could not do this, and Mary, the key to the barn still in her hands, followed her out. They went through the cold kitchen where the refrigerator and the ironing board and the clothes bars and all the familiar things stood in the dark. To Mary these were sunk in a great obscurity and insignificance, and even Jenny being there was unimportant beside the thing that her letter had brought to think about. They stepped out into the clear, glittering night, with its clean, white world, and its clean, dark sky on which some story was written in stars. Capella was shining almost overhead — and another star was hanging bright in the east, as if the east were always a dawning place for some new star.

"Mary!" said Jenny, there in the dark.

"Yes," Mary answered.

"You know I said I just couldn't bear not to have any Christmas — *this* Christmas?"

"Yes," Mary said.

"Did you know why?"

"I thought because it's your and Bruce's first —"

"No," Jenny said, "that isn't all why. It's something else."

She slipped her arm within Mary's and stood silent. And, Mary still not understanding, —

"It's somebody else," Jenny said faintly.

Mary stirred, turned to her in the dimness.

"Why, Jenny!" she said.

"Soon," said Jenny.

The two women stood for a moment, Jenny saying a little, Mary quiet.

"It'll be late in December," Jenny finished. "That seems so wonderful to me — so wonderful. Late in December, like —"

CHRISTMAS 71

The cold came pricking about them, and Jenny moved to go. Mary, the shawled figure on the upper step, looked down on the shawled figure below her, and abruptly spoke.

"It's funny," Mary said, "that you should tell me that — now. I haven't told you what's in my letter."

"What was?" asked Jenny.

Mary told her. "They want I should have the little boy," she ended it.

"Oh . . ." Jenny said. "Mary! How wonderful for you! Why, it's almost next as wonderful as mine!"

Mary hesitated for a breath. But she was profoundly stirred by what Jenny had told her — the first time, so far as she could recall, that news like this had ever come to her directly, as a secret and a marvel. News of the village births usually came in gossip, in commiseration, in suspicion. Falling as did this confidence in a time when she was re-living her old hope, when Adam's boy stood outside her threshold, the moment quite suddenly put on its real significance.

"We can plan together," Jenny was saying. "Ain't it wonderful?"

"Ain't it?" Mary said then, simply, and kissed Jenny, when Jenny came and kissed her. Then Jenny went away.

Mary went on to the barn, and opened the door, and listened. She had brought no lantern, but the soft stillness within needed no vigilance. The hay smell from the loft and the mangers, the even breath of the cows, the quiet safety of the place, met her. She was wondering at herself, but she was struggling not at all. It was as if concerning the little boy, something had decided for her, in a soft, fierce rush of feeling not her own. She had committed herself to Jenny almost without will. But Mary felt no exultation, and the weight within her did not lift.

"I really couldn't do anything else but take him, I s'pose," she thought. "I wonder what'll come on me next?"

All the while, she was conscious of the raw smell of the clover in the hay of the mangers, as if something of Summer were there in the cold.

VI

MARY CHAVAH sent her letter of blunt directions concerning her sister's headstone and the few belongings which her sister had wished her to have. The last lines of the letter were about the boy.

"Send the little one along. I am not the one, but I don't know what else to tell you to do with him. Let me know when to expect him, and put his name in with his things — I can't remember his right name."

When the answer came from John Blood, a fortnight later, it said that a young fellow of those parts was starting back home shortly to spend Christmas, and would take charge of the child as far as the City, and there put him on his train for Old Trail Town. She would be notified just what day to expect him, and John knew how glad his mother would have been and his father too, and he was her grateful Nephew. P. S. He would send some money every month "toward him."

The night after she received this letter, Mary lay long awake, facing what it was going to mean to have him there: to have a child there.

She recalled what she had heard other women say about it, — stray utterances, made with the burdened look that hid a secret complacency, a kind of pleased freemasonry in a universal lot.

"The children bring so much sand into the house. You'd think it was horses."

". . . the center table looks loaded and ready to start half the time . . . but I can't help it, with the children's books and truck."

". . . never would have another house built

without a coat closet. The children's cloaks and caps and rubbers litter up everything."

" . . . every one of their knees out, and their underclothes outgrown, and their waists soiled, the whole time. And I do try so hard . . ."

Now with all these bewilderments she was to have to do. She wondered if she would know how to dress him. Once she had watched Mis' Winslow dress a child, and she remembered what unexpected places Mis' Winslow had buttoned—buttonholes that went *up and down* in the skirt bands, and so on. Armholes might be too small and garters too tight, and how was one ever to know? If it were a little girl now . . . but a little boy. . . . What would she talk to him about while they ate together?

She lay in the dark and planned — with no pleasure, but merely because she always planned

"HE STOOD LOOKING AT IT FROM PART WAY ACROSS THE ROAD"

everything, her dress, her baking, what she would say to this one and that. She would put up a stove in the back parlour, and give him the room "off." She was glad that the parlour was empty and clean — "no knick-knacks for a boy to knock around," she found herself thinking. And a child would like the bedroom wallpaper, with the owl border. When Summer came he could have the room over the dining room, with the kitchen roof sloping away from it where he could dry his hazelnuts — she had thought of the pasture hazelnuts, first thing. There were a good many things a boy would like about the place: the bird house where the martins always built, the hens, the big hollow tree, the pasture ant hill. . . . She would have to find out the things he liked to eat. She would have to help him with his lessons — she could do that for only a little while, until he would be too old to need her. Then maybe there would come the time when he would ask her things that she would not know. . . .

She fell asleep wondering how he would look. Already, not from any impatience to have this done, but because that was the way in which she worked, she had his room in order; and her picture of his father was by the mirror, the young face of his father. Something faded had been written below the picture, and this she had painstakingly rubbed away before she set the picture in its place. Next day, while she was working on Mis' Jane Moran's bead basque that was to be cut over and turned, she laid it aside and cut out a jacket pattern, and a plaited waist pattern — just to see if she could. These she rolled up impatiently and stuffed away in her pattern bookcase.

"I knew how to do them all the while, and I never knew I knew," she thought with annoyed surprise. "I s'pose I'll waste a lot of time pottering over him."

It was so that she spent the weeks until the letter came telling her what day the child would start. On the afternoon of the day the letter came, she went down town to the Amos Ames Emporium to buy a washbasin and pitcher for the room she meant the little boy to have. She stood looking at a basin with a row of brown dogs around the rim, when over her shoulder Mis' Abby Winslow spoke.

"You ain't buying a Christmas present for anybody, are you?" she asked warningly.

Mary started guiltily and denied it.

"Well, what in time do you want with dogs on the basin?" Mis' Winslow demanded.

Almost against her own wish, Mary told her. Mis' Winslow was one of those whose faces are invariable forerunners of the sort of thing they are going to say. With eyebrows, eyes, forehead, head, and voice she took the news.

"He is! Forever and ever more. When's he going to get here?"

"Week after next," Mary said listlessly. "It's an awful responsibility, ain't it — taking a child so?"

Mis' Winslow's face abruptly rejected its own anxious lines and let the eyes speak for it.

"I always think children is like air," she said; "you never realize how hard they're pressing down on you — but you do know you can't live without them."

Mary looked at her, her own face not lighting.

"I'd rather go along like I am," she said; "I'm used to myself the way I am."

"Mary Chavah!" said Mis' Winslow, sharply, "a vegetable sprouts. Can't you? Is these stocking caps made so's they won't ravel?" she inquired capably of Abel Ames. "These are real good value, Mary," she added kindly. "Better su'prise the little thing with one of these. A red one."

Mary counted over her money, and bought the red stocking cap and the basin with the puppies. Then she went into the street. The sense of oppression, of striving, that had seldom left her since that night in the stable, made the day a thing to be borne, to be breasted. The air was thick with snow, and in the whiteness the dreary familiarity of the drug store, the meat market, the post office, the Simeon Buck Dry Goods Exchange, smote her with a passion to escape from them all, to breed new familiars, to get free of the thing that she had said she would do.

"And I could," she thought; "I could telegraph to John not to send him. But Jenny — she can't. I don't see how she stands it. . . ."

The thought may have been why, instead of

going home, she went to see Jenny. A neighbor was in the sitting room with Mrs. Wing. Jenny met Mary at the kitchen door and stood against a background of clothes drying on lines stretched indoors.

"Don't you want to come upstairs?" Jenny said. "There ain't a fire up there — but I can show you the things."

She had put them all in the bottom drawer, as women always do; and, as women always do, had laid them so that all the lace and embroidery and pink ribbons possible showed in a flutter when the drawer was opened. Jenny took the things out, one at a time, unfolded, discussed, compared, with all the tireless zeal of a robin with a straw in its mouth or of a tree, blossoming. "Smell of them," Jenny bade her. "Honestly, wouldn't you know by the smell who they are for?" "I donno but you would," Mary admitted awkwardly, and marveled dumbly at the newness Jenny was feeling in that which, after all, was not new!

When these things were all out, a little tissue-paper parcel was left lying in the drawer.

"There's one more," Mary said.

Jenny flushed, hesitated, lifted it.

"That's nothing," she said; "before I came I made some little things for its Christmas. I thought maybe it would come first, and we'd have the Christmas in my room, and I made some little things — just for fun, you know. But it won't be fair to do it now, with the whole town so set against our having any Christmas. Mary, it just seems as though I had to have a Christmas this year!"

"Oh, well," said Mary, "the baby'll be your Christmas. The town can't help that, I guess."

"I know," Jenny flashed back brightly,

"you and I have got the best of them, haven't we? We've each got one present coming, anyway."

"I s'pose we have . . ." Mary said.

She looked at Jenny's Christmas things — a ribbon rattle, a crocheted cap, a first picture book, a cascade of colored rings — and then in grim humour at Jenny.

"It'll never miss its Christmas," she said dryly.

"Don't you think so?" said Jenny, soberly. "I donno. It seems as if it'd be kind o' lonesome to get born around Christmas and not find any going on."

She put the things away, and closed the drawer. For no appreciable reason, she kept it locked, and the key under the bureau cover.

"Do you know yet when yours is coming?" Jenny asked, as she rose.

"Week after next," Mary repeated, — "two

weeks from last night," she confessed, "if he comes straight through."

"I think," said Jenny, "I think mine will be here — before then."

When they reached the foot of the stair, Mary unexpectedly refused to go in the sitting room.

"No," she said, "I must be getting home. I just come out for a minute, anyway. I'm — I'm much obliged for what you showed me," she added, and hesitated. "I've got his room fixed up real nice. There's owls on the wall paper and puppies on the washbasin," she said. "Come in when you can and see it."

It was almost dusk when Mary reached home. While she was passing the billboard at the corner — a flare of yellow letters, as if Colour and the Alphabet had united to breed a monster — she heard children shouting. A block away, and across the street, coming home from Rolleston's hill where they had been coasting, were Bennet and Gussie Bates, little Emily, Tab Winslow, and Pep. Nearly every day of snow they passed her house. She always heard them talking, and usually she heard, across at the corner, the click of the penny-in-the-slot machine, which no child seemed able to pass without pulling. To-night, as she heard them coming, Mary fumbled in her purse. Three, four, five pennies she found and ran across the street and dropped them in the slot machine, and gained her own door before the children came. She stood at her dark threshold, and listened. She had not reckoned in vain. One of the children pushed down on the rod, in the child's eternal hope of magic, and when magic came and three, four, five chocolates dropped obediently in their hands, Mary listened to what they said. It was not much, and it was not very coherent, but it was wholly intelligible.

"Look at!" shrieked Bennet, who had made the magic.

"*Did* it?" cried Gussie, and repeated the operation.

"It — it — it never!" said Tab Winslow, at the third.

"Make it again — make it again!" cried little Emily, and they did.

"Gorry," observed Pep, in ecstasy.

When it would give no more, they divided with the other children and ran on, their red mittens and mufflers flaming in the snow. Mary stood staring after them for a moment, then she closed her door.

"I wonder what made me do that," she thought.

In her dining room she mended the fire without taking off her hat. It was curious, she reflected; here was this room looking the way it looked, and away off there was the little fellow who had never seen the room; and in a little while he would be calling this room home, and looking for his books and his mittens, and knowing it better than any other place in the world. And there was Jenny, with that bottom drawerful, and pretty soon somebody that now was not, would be, and would be wearing the drawerful and calling Jenny "mother," and would know her better than any one else in the world. Mary could not imagine that little boy of Lily's getting used to her — Mary — and calling her — well, what would he call her? She hadn't thought of that. . . .

"Bother," thought Mary Chavah, "there's going to be forty nuisances about it that I s'pose I haven't even thought of yet."

She stood by the window. She had not lighted the lamp, so the world showed white, not black. Snow makes outdoors look big, she thought. But it was big — what a long journey it was to Idaho. Suppose . . . something happened to the man he was to travel with. John Blood was only a boy; he would probably put the child's name and her address in the little traveler's pocket, and these would be lost. The child was hardly old enough to remember what to do. He would go astray, and none of them would ever know what had become of him . . . and what would become of him? She saw him and his bundle of clothes alone in the station in the City. . . .

She turned from the window and mechanically mended the fire again. She drew down the window shade and went to the coat closet to hang away her wraps. Then abruptly she took up her purse, counted out the money in the firelight, and went out the door and down the street in the dusk, and into the post office, which was also the telegraph office, — one which the little town owed to Ebenezer Rule, and it a rival to the other telegraph office at the station.

"How much does it cost to send a telegram?" she demanded. "Idaho," she answered the man's question, flushing at her omission.

While the man, Affer by name, laboriously looked it up, — covering incredible little dirty figures with an incredibly big dirty forefinger, — Mary stood staring at the list of names tacked below the dog-eared Christmas Notice. She remembered that she had not yet signed it herself. She asked for a pencil — causing confusion to the little figures and delay to the big finger — and, while she waited, wrote her name. "A good, sensible move," she thought, as she signed.

When Affer gave her the rate, thrusting finger and figures jointly beneath the bars, — solicitous of his own accuracy, — Mary filed her message. It was to John Blood, and it read: —

"Be sure you tie his tag on him good."

VII

EBENEZER RULE had meant to go to the City before cold weather came. He had there a small and decent steam-warmed flat where he boiled his own eggs and made his own coffee, read his newspapers and kept his counsel, descending nightly to the ground-floor café to dine on ambiguous dishes at tables of other bank swallows who nested in the same cliff. But as the days went by, he found himself staying on in Old Trail Town, with this excuse and that, offered by himself to himself. As, for example, that in the factory there were old account books that he must go through. And having put off this task from day to day and finding at last nothing more to dally with, he set out one morning for the ancient building down in that part of the village which was older than the rest and was where his business was conducted when it was conducted.

It had snowed in the night, and Buff Miles, who drove the village snowplow, was also driver of "the 'bus." So on the morning after a snowfall, the streets always lay buried thick until after the 8.10 Express came in; and since on the morning following a snowfall the 8.10 Express was always late, Old Trail Town lay locked in a kind of circular argument, and everybody stayed indoors or stepped high through drifts. The direct way to the factory was virtually untrodden, and Ebenezer made a detour through the business street in search of some semblance of a "track."

The light of a Winter morning is not kind, only just. It is just to the sky and discovers it to be dominant; to trees, and their lines are seen to be alive, like leaves; to folk, and no disguise avails. Summer gives complements and accessories to the good things in a human face. Winter affords nothing save disclosure. In the uncompromising cleanness of that wash of Winter light, Ebenezer Rule was himself, for anybody to see. Looking like countless other men, lean, alert, preoccupied, his tall figure stooped, his smooth, pale face like a photograph too much retouched, this commonplace man took his place in the day almost as one of its externals. With that glorious pioneer trio, mineral, vegetable and animal; and with intellect, that worthy tool, he did his day's work. His face was one that had never asked itself, say, of a Winter morning: *What else?* And the Winter light searched him pitilessly to find that question somewhere in him.

Before the Simeon Buck North American Dry Goods Exchange, Simeon Buck himself had just finished shoveling his walk, and stood wiping his snow shovel with an end of his muffler. When he saw Ebenezer, he shook the muffler at him, and then, over his left shoulder, jabbed the air with his thumb.

"Look at here," he said, his head reënforcing his gesture toward his show window, "look what I done this morning. Nice little touch — eh?"

In the show window of the Exchange — Dry Goods Exchange was just the name of it for the store carried everything — a hodgepodge of canned goods, lace curtains, kitchen utensils, wax figures, and bird cages had been ranged round a center table of golden oak. On the table stood a figure that was as familiar to Old Trail Town as was its fire engine and its sprinkling cart. Like these, appearing intermittently, the figure had seized on the imagination of the children and grown in association until it belonged to everybody, by sheer use and wont. It was a *papier-mâché* Santa Claus, three feet high, white-bearded, gray-gowned, with tall pointed cap — rather the more sober Saint Nicholas of earlier days than the rollicking, red-garbed Saint Nick of now. Only, whereas for years he had graced the window of the Exchange, bearing over his shoulder a little bough of green for a Christmas tree, this season he stood treeless, and instead bore on his shoulder a United States flag. On a placard below him Simeon had laboriously lettered: —

> HIGH COST OF LIVING
> AND TOO MUCH FUSS
> MAKES FOLKS WANT A
> SANE CHRISTMAS
> ME TOO.   S. C.

"Ain't that neat?" said Simeon.

Ebenezer looked. "What's the flag for?" he inquired dryly.

"Well," said Simeon, "he had to carry something. I thought of a toy gun — but that didn't seem real appropriate. A Japanese umbrella wasn't exactly in season, seems though. A flag was about the only thing I could think of to have him hold. A flag is always kind of tasty, don't you think?"

"Oh, it's harmless," Ebenezer said, "harmless."

"No hustling business," Simeon pursued, "can be contented with just *not* doing something. It ain't enough not to have no Christmas. You've got to find something that'll express nothing, and express it forcible. In business, a minus sign," said Simeon, "is as good as a plus, if you can keep it whirling round and round."

This Ebenezer mulled and chuckled over as he went on down the street. He wondered what the Emporium would do to keep up with the Exchange. But in the Emporium window

CHRISTMAS

there was nothing save the usual mill-end display for the winter white goods sale.

Ebenezer opened the store door and put his head in.

"Hey," he shouted at Abel, back at the desk, "can't you keep up with Simeon's window?"

Abel came down the aisle between the lengths of white stuff plaited into folds at either side. The fire had just been kindled in the stove, and the air in the store was still frosty. Abel, in his overcoat, was blowing on his fingers.

"I ain't much of any heart to," said he, "but the night before Christmas I guess'll do about right for mine."

"What'll you put up?" Ebenezer asked, closing the door behind him.

"Well, sir," said Abel, "I ain't made up my mind full yet. But I'll be billblowed if I'm going to let Christmas go by without saying something about it in the window."

"Night before Christmas'll be too late to advertise anything," said Ebenezer. "If I was in trade," he said, half closing his eyes, "I'd fill my window up with useful articles — caps and mittens and stockings and warm underwear and dishes and toothbrushes. And I'd say: 'Might as well afford these on what you saved out of Christmas.' You'd ought to get all the advertising you can out of any situation."

Abel shook his head.

"I ain't much on such," he said lightly — and then looked intently at Ebenezer. "Jenny's been buying quite a lot here for her Christmas," he said.

Ebenezer was blank. "Jenny?" he said. "Jenny Wing? I heard she was here. I ain't seen her. Is she bound to keep Christmas anyhow?"

"Just white goods, it was," said Abel, briefly.

Ebenezer frowned his lack of understanding.

"I shouldn't think her and Bruce had much of anything to buy anything with," he said. "I s'pose you know," he added, "that Bruce, the young beggar, quit working for me in the City after the — the failure? Threw up his job with me, and took God knows what to do."

Abel nodded gravely. All Old Trail Town knew that, and honoured Bruce for it.

"Headstrong couple," Ebenezer added. "So Jenny's bent on having Christmas, no matter what the town decides, is she?" he added, "it's like her, the minx."

"I don't think it was planned that way," Abel said simply; "she's only buying white goods," he repeated. And, Ebenezer still staring, "Surely you know what Jenny's come home for?" Abel said.

A moment or two later Ebenezer was out on the street again, his face turned toward the factory. He was aware that Abel caught open the door behind him and called after him, "Whenever you get ready to sell me that there star glass, you know...." Ebenezer answered something, but his responses were so often guttural and indistinguishable that his will to reply was regarded as nominal, anyway. He also knew that now, just before him, Buff Miles was proceeding with the snowplow, cutting a firm, white way, smooth and sparkling for soft treading, momentarily bordered by a feathery flux, that tumbled and heaped and then lay quiet in a glitter of crystals. But his thought went on without these things and without his will.

Bruce's baby! It would be a Rule, too. .... the third generation, the third generation. And accustomed as he was to relate every experience to himself, measure it, value it by its own value to him, the effect of his reflection was at first single: The third generation of Rules. *Was he as old as that?*

It seemed only yesterday that Bruce had been a boy, in a blue necktie to match his eyes, and shoes which for some reason he always put on wrong, so that the buttons were on the inside. Bruce's baby. Good heavens! It had been a shock when Bruce graduated from the high school, a shock when he had married, but his baby . . . it was incredible that he himself should be so old as that.

. . . This meant, then, that if Malcolm had lived, Malcolm might have had a child now. . . .

Ebenezer had not meant to think that. It was as if the Thought came and spoke to him. He never allowed himself to think of that other life of his, when his wife, Letty, and his son Malcolm had been living. Nobody in Old Trail Town ever heard him speak of them or had ever been answered when Ebenezer had been spoken to concerning them. A high white shaft in the cemetery marked the two graves. All about them doors had been closed. But with the thought of this third generation, the doors all opened. He looked along ways that he had forgotten.

As he went he was unconscious, as he was always unconscious, of the little street. He saw the market square, not as the heart of the town, but as a place for buying and selling, and the little shops were to him not ways of providing the town with life, but ways of providing their keepers with a livelihood. Beyond these was a familiar setting, arranged that day with white background and heaped roofs and laden boughs, the houses standing side by side, like human beings. There they were, like the chorus to the thing he was thinking about. They were all thinking about it, too. Every one of them knew what he knew. Yet he never saw the bond, but he thought they were only the places where men lived who had been his factory hands and would be so yet if he had not cut them away: Ben Torrey, shoveling off his front walk with his boy sweeping behind him; August Muir, giving his little girl a ride on the snow shovel; Nettie Hatch, clearing the ice out of her mail box, while her sister — the lame one — watched from her chair by the window, interested as in a real event. Ebenezer spoke to them from some outpost of consciousness which his thought did not pass. The little street was not there, as it was never there for him, as an entity. It was merely a street. And the little town was not an entity. It was merely where he lived. He went behind Buff Miles and the snowplow — as he always went — as if space had been created for folk to live in one at a time, and as if this were his own turn.

When he reached the bend from the Old Trail to the road where the factory was, he understood at last that he had been hearing a song sung over a great many times.

> "... *One for the way it all begun,*
> *Two for the way it all has run,*
> *What three'll be for I do forget,*
> *But what's to be has not been yet. ...*
> *So holly and mistletoe,*
> *So holly and mistletoe,*
> *So holly and mistletoe,*
> *Over and over and over, oh.*"

Buff, who was singing it, looked over his shoulder, and nodded.

"They said you can't have no Christmas on Christmas Day," he observed, grinning, "but I ain't heard nothing to prevent singing Christmas carols right up to the day that is the day."

Ebenezer halted.

"How old are you?" he abruptly demanded of Buff — whom he had known from Buff's boyhood.

"Thirty-three," said Buff, "dum it."

"You and Bruce about the same age, ain't you?" said Ebenezer.

Buff nodded.

"Well," said Ebenezer, "well . . . " and stood looking at him. Malcolm would have been his age, too.

"Going down to the factory, are you?" Buff said. "Wait a bit. I'll hike on down ahead of you."

He turned the snowplow down the factory road, as if he were making a triumphal progress, fashioning his snow borders with all the freedom of some sculpturing wind on summer clouds.

"One for the way it all begun,
 Two for the way it all has run. . . ."

he sang to the soft push and thud and clank of his going. He swept a circle in front of the little house that was the factory office, as if he had prepared the setting for a great event; and Ebenezer, following in the long, bright path, stepped into the hall of the house.

For thirty years he had been accustomed to enter the little house with his mind ready to receive its interior of desks and shelves and safes and files. To-day, quite unexpectedly, as he opened the door, the thing that was in his mind was a hall stair with a red carpet, and a parlour adjoining with figured stuff at the windows and a coal fire in the stove. . . . And thirty-five years ago it had been that way, when he and his wife and child had lived in the little house where his business was then just starting at a machine set up in the woodshed. As his project had grown and his factory had arisen in the neighbouring lots, the family had moved farther up in the town. Remembrance had been divorced from this place for decades.

CHRISTMAS

To-day, without warning, it waited for him on the threshold.

He had asked his bookkeeper to meet him there, but the man had not yet arrived. So Ebenezer himself kindled a fire in the rusty office stove, in the room where the figured curtains had been. The old account books that he wanted were not here on the shelves, nor in the cupboards of the cold adjoining rooms. They dated so far back that they had been filed away upstairs. He had not been upstairs in years, and his first impulse was to send his bookkeeper, when he should appear. But this, after all, was not Ebenezer's way; and he went up the stairs himself.

Each upper room was like some one unconscious in stupor or death, and still as distinct in personality as if in some ancient activity. There was the shelf he had put up in their room, the burned place on the floor where he had tipped over a lamp, tattered shreds of the paper she had hung to surprise him, the little storeroom which they had cleared out for Malcolm when he was old enough, and whose door had had to be kept closed because innumerable uncaged birds lived there. . . .

When he had gone through the piles of account books in a closet and those he sought were not found among them, he remembered the trunkful up in the tiny loft. He let down from the passage ceiling the ladder he had once hung there, and climbed up to the little roof recess.

Light entered through four broken panes of skylight. It fell in a faint rug on the dusty floor. The roof sloped sharply, and the trunks and boxes had been pressed back to the rim of the place. Ebenezer put his hands out, groping. They touched an edge of something that swayed. He laid hold of it and drew it out and set down on the faint rug of light a small wooden hobbyhorse.

He stood staring at it, remembering it as clearly as if some one had set before him the old white gate which he bestrode in his own boyhood. It was Malcolm's hobbyhorse, dappled gray, the tail and the mane missing and the paint worn off — and tenderly licked off — his nose. When they had moved to the other house, he had bought the boy a pony, and this horse had been left behind. Something else stirred in his memory, the name by which Malcolm had used to call his hobbyhorse, some ringing name . . . but he had forgotten. He thrust the thing back where it had been and went on with his search for the account books.

By the time he had found them and had got down again in the office, the bookkeeper was there, keeping up the fire and uttering, with some acumen, comments on the obvious aspects of the weather, of the climate, of the visible universe. The bookkeeper was a young man, very ready to agree with Ebenezer for the sake of future favour, but with the wistfulness of all industrial machines constructed by men from human potentialities. Also, he had a cough and thin hands and a little family and no job.

"Get to work on this book," Ebenezer bade him; "it's the one that began the business."

The man opened the book, put it to his nearsighted eyes, frowned, and glanced up at Ebenezer.

"I don't think it seems . . ." he began doubtfully.

"Well, don't think," said Ebenezer, sharply; "that's not needful. Read the first entries."

The bookkeeper read:—

"ACROSS THE STILL FIELDS CAME FLASHING
THE POINT OF FLAME."

Picking hops (4 days) $1.00
Sewing (Mrs. Shackell) 60
Egg money (3¼ dozen) 75
Winning puzzle 2.50
                                 ─────
                                 $4.86

Disbursed:

Kitchen roller . . . . $ .10
Coffee mill 50
Shoes for M. 1.25
Water colors for M. 25
Suit for M. 2.00
Gloves — mc 50
                                ─────
                                $4.75

Cash on hand: 11 cents.

The bookkeeper paused again. Ebenezer, frowning, reached for the book. In his wife's fine faded writing were her accounts — after the eleven cents was a funny little face with which she had been wont to illustrate her letters. Ebenezer stared, grunted, turned to the last page of the book. There, in bold figures, the other way of the leaf, was his own accounting. He remembered now — he had kept his first books in the back of the account book that she had used for the house.

Ebenezer glanced sharply at his bookkeeper. To his annoyance, the man was smiling with perfect comprehension and sympathy. Ebenezer averted his eyes, and the bookkeeper felt dimly that he had been guilty of an indelicacy toward his employer, and hastened to cover it.

"Family life does cling to a man, sir," he said.

"Do you find it so?" said Ebenezer, dryly. "Read, please."

At noon Ebenezer walked home alone through the melting snow. And the Thought that he did not think, but that spoke to him without his knowing, said: —

"Winning a puzzle — Two Dollars and a half. She never told me she tried to earn a little something that way."

VIII

"If we took the day before Christmas an' had it for Christmas," observed Tab Winslow, "would that hurt?"

"Eat your oatmeal," said Mis' Winslow, in the immemorial manner of adults.

"Would it, would it, would it?" persisted Tab, in the immemorial manner of youth.

"And have Theophilus Thistledown for dinner that day instead?" Mis' Winslow suggested with diplomacy.

On which Tab ate his oatmeal in silence.

But, like adults immemorially, Mis' Winslow bore far more the adult manner than its heart. After breakfast she stood staring out the pantry window at the sparrows on the bird box.

"It looks like Mary Chavah was going to be the only one in Trail Town to have any Christmas after all," she thought, "that little boy coming to her, so."

He was coming week after next, Mary had said, and Mis' Winslow had heard no word about it from anybody else. When "the biggest of the work" of the forenoon was finished, Mis' Winslow ran down the road to Ellen Bourne's. In Old Trail Town they always speak of it as running down, or in, or over, in the morning, with an unconscious suiting of terms to informalities.

Ellen was cleaning her silver. She had "six of each" — six knives, six forks, six spoons, all plated and seldom used, pewter with black handles serving for every day. The silver was cleaned often, though it was never on the table, save for company, and there never had been any company since Ellen had lost her little boy from fever. Having no articulateness and having no other outlet for emotion, she fed her grief by small abstentions: no guests, no diversions, no snatches of song about her work. Yet she was sane enough, and normal, only in dearth of sane and normal outlets for emotion, for energy, for personality, she had taken these strange directions for yet unharnessed forces.

"Mercy," observed Mis' Winslow, warming her hands at the cooking stove, "you got more energy."

". . . than family, I guess you mean," Ellen Bourne finished. Ellen was little and fair, with slightly drooping head, and eyebrows curved to a childlike reflectiveness.

"Well, I got consider'ble more family than I got energy," said Mis' Winslow, "so I guess we even it up. Seven-under-fifteen eats up energy like so much air."

"Hey, king and country," said Ellen's old father, whittling by the fire, "you got family enough, Ellen. You got your hands full of us." He rubbed his hands through his thin upstanding silver hair on his little pink head, and his fine, pink face took on the look of father which rarely intruded, now, on his settled look of old man.

"I donno what she'd do," said Ellen's mother, "with any more around here to pick up after. We're cluttered up enough, as it is." She was an old lady of whose outlines you took notice before your attention lay further upon her — angled waist, chin, lips, forehead, put on her a succession of zigzags. But her eyes were awake, and it was to be seen that she did not mean what she said and that she was looking anxiously at Ellen in the hope of having deceived her daughter. Ellen smiled at her brightly, and was not deceived.

"I keep pretty busy," she said.

Mis' Abby Winslow, who was not deceived either, hastened to the subject of Mary.

"I should think Mary Chavah had enough to do, too," she said, "but she's going to take Lily's little boy. Had you heard?"

"No," Ellen said, and stopped shaving silver polish.

"He's coming in two weeks," Mis' Winslow imparted; "she told me so herself. She's got his room fixed up with owls on the wall paper. She's bought him a washbasin with a rim of puppies, and a red stocking cap. I saw her."

"How old is he?" Ellen asked, and worked again.

"I never thought to ask her," Mis' Winslow confessed; "he must be quite a little fellow. But he's coming alone from some place out West."

"Hey, king and country," Ellen's father said; "I'd hate to have a boy come here, with my head the way it is."

"And keeping the house all upset," Ellen's mother said, and asked Mis' Winslow some question about Mary; and when she turned to Ellen again, "Why, Ellen Bourne," she said, "you've shaved up every bit of that cleaning polish and we're most done cleaning."

Ellen was looking at Mis' Winslow: "If you see her," Ellen said, "you ask her if I can't do anything to help."

Later in the day, happening in at Mis' Mortimer Bates's, Mis' Winslow found Mis' Moran there before her, and asked what they had heard "about Mary Chavah." Something in that word "about" pricks curiosity its sharpest. "Have you heard about Mary Chavah?" "It's too bad about Mary Chavah." "Isn't it queer about Mary Chavah?"—each of these is like setting flame to an edge of tissue. Omit "about" from the language, and you abate most gossip. At Mis' Winslow's phrase, both women's eyebrows curved to another arc.

Mis' Winslow told them.

"Ain't that nice?" said Mis' Moran, wholeheartedly; "I couldn't bring up another, not with my back. But I'm glad Mary's going to know what it is. . . ."

Mis' Mortimer Bates was glad, too, but being by nature a nonconformist, she took exception.

"It's an awful undertaking for a singlehanded woman," she observed.

But this sort of thing she said almost unconsciously, and the other two women regarded it with no more alarm than any other reflex.

"It's no worse starting single-handed than being left single-handed," offered Mis' Winslow somewhat ambiguously. "Lots does that's thrifty."

"Seems as if we could do a little something to help her get ready, seem's though," Mis' Moran suggested; "I donno what."

"I thought I'd slip over after supper and ask her, " Mis' Winslow said; "maybe I'd best go now — and come back and tell you what she says."

Mis' Winslow found Mary Chavah sitting by her pattern bookcase, cutting out a pattern. Mary's face was flushed and her eyes were bright, and she went on with her pattern, thrilled by it as by any other creating.

"I just thought of this," Mary explained, looking vaguely at her visitor. "It come to me like a flash when I was working on Mis' Bates's basque. Will you wait just a minute, and then I'll explain it out to you."

Without invitation, Mis' Winslow laid aside

her coat and waited, watching Mary curiously. She was cutting and folding and pinning her tissue paper, oblivious of any presence. Alarm, suspense, doubt, solution, triumph, came and went, and neither woman was conscious that the flame of creation burned and breathed in the room as truly as if the product were to be acknowledged.

"There!" Mary cried at last. "See it — can't you see it? — in gray wool?"

It was the pattern for a boy's topcoat, cunningly cut in new lines of seam and revers, with a pocket, a bit of braid, a line of buttons laid in as delicately as the factors in any other good composition. Mis' Winslow inevitably recognized its utility, exclaimed, and wondered.

"Mary Chavah! How did you know how to do things for children?"

"How did you know how?" Mary inquired coolly.

"Why, I've had 'em," Mis' Winslow offered simply.

"Do you honestly think that makes any difference?" Mary asked.

Mis' Winslow gasped, in the immemorial belief that the physical basis of motherhood is the guarantee of both spiritual and physical equipment.

"Could you have cut out that coat?" Mary asked.

Mis' Winslow shook her head. She was of those whose genius is for cutting over.

"Well," said Mary, "I could. It ain't having 'em that teaches you to do for 'em. You either know how, or you don't know how. That's all."

Mis' Winslow reflected that she could never make Mary understand — though any mother, she thought complacently, would know in a minute. The cutting of the coat did give her pause; but then, she summed it up, coat included, "Mary was queer" — and let it go at that.

"I didn't know," Mis' Winslow said then, "but what I could help you some about the little boy's coming. Seven-under-fifteen does teach you something, you've got to allow. Mebbe I could tell you something, now and then. Or if we could do anything to help you get ready for him . . ."

"Oh," said Mary, in swift penitence, "thank you, Mis' Winslow. After he comes, maybe. But these things now I don't mind doing. The real nuisance'll come afterwards, I s'pose."

Mis' Winslow smiled in soft triumph.

"*Nuisance!*" she said. "That's what I meant comes to you by having 'em. You don't think so much of the nuisance part as you did before."

"Then you don't look the thing in the

face," said Mary, calmly. "That's all about that."

"Well," Mis' Winslow said pacifically, "when's he coming?"

"A week from Tuesday. A week from to-morrow," Mary told her.

Mis' Winslow looked at her intently, with the light of calculation in her narrowed eyes.

"A week from Tuesday," she said. "A week from Tuesday," she repeated. *"A week from Tuesday!"* she exclaimed. "Why, Mary Chavah. That's Christmas Eve."

It was some matter of recipes that was absorbing Mis' Bates and Mis' Moran when Mis' Winslow breathlessly returned to them. They were deep in tradition, and in method, its buttonhole relation. During the weary period when nutrition has been one of the two great problems the tremendous impulse that has nourished the world was alive in the faces of the two women, a kind of creative fire, such as had burned in Mary at the cutting of her pattern. Asparagus escalloped with toast crumbs and butter was for the moment symbol of all humanity's will to keep alive.

"Ladies," said Mis' Winslow, with no other preface, "what do you think? Mary Chavah's little boy is coming from Idaho with a tag on, and when do you s'pose he's going to get here? Christmas Eve."

"Christmas Eve," repeated Mis' Bates, whose mind never lightly forsook old ways or embraced a contretemps; "what a funny time to travel."

"Likely catch the croup and be down sick on Mary's hands the first thing," said Mis' Moran. "It's a pity it ain't the Spring of the year."

Mis' Winslow looked at them searchingly to see if her thought too far outdistanced theirs.

"What struck me all of a heap," she said, "is his getting here then. *That* night. Christmas Eve."

The three woman looked at one another.

"That's so," Mis' Moran said.

"Him — that child," Mis' Winslow put it, "getting here Christmas Eve, used to Christmas all his life, ten to one knowing in his head what he hopes he'll get. And no Christmas. And him with no mother. And her only a month or so dead."

"Well," said Mis' Mortimer Bates, "it's too bad it's happened so. But it has happened so. You have to say that to your life quite often, I notice. I don't know anything to do but to say it now."

Mis' Winslow had not taken off her cloak. She sat on the edge of her chair, with her hands deep in its pockets, her black knit "fascinator" fallen back from her hair. She was looking down at her cloth overshoes, and she went on speaking as if she had hardly heard what Mis' Bates had interposed.

"He'll get in on the express," she said; "Mary said so. She don't have to go to the City to meet him. The man he travels with is going to put him on the train in the City. The little fellow'll get here after dark. After dark on Christmas Eve."

"And no time for anybody to warn him that there won't be any Christmas waiting for him," Mis' Moran observed thoughtfully.

"And like enough he'll bring a little something for Mary for a present," Mis' Winslow went on. "How'll she feel *then?*"

"Ain't it too bad it ain't last year?" Mis' Moran mourned. "Everything comes too late or too soon or not at all or else too much so, 'seems though."

Mis' Bates's impulse to nonconformity had

not prevented her forehead from being drawn in their common sympathy; but it was a sympathy that saw no practical way out and existed tamely as a high window and not as a wide door.

"Well," she said, "Mary ain't exactly the one to see it so. You'll never get her to feel bad about anybody not having a Christmas. I donno, if it was any other year, as she'd be planning any different."

"No," said Mis' Winslow, thoughtfully, "Mary won't do anything. But we could."

Mis' Bates's forehead took alarm — the alarm of the sympathetic hearer who is challenged to be doer.

"*Do?*" she repeated. "You can't go back on the paper at this late day. And you can't give him a Christmas and every other of our children not have any just because we're their parents and still living. There ain't a thing to do."

K

Mis' Winslow's eyes were still on her overshoes. "I don't believe there's *never* 'not a thing' to do," she said, "I don't believe it."

Mis' Bates looked scandalized. "That's nonsense," she said sharply, "and it's sacrilegious besides. When God means a thing to happen, there's not a thing to do. What about earthquakes and — and cancers?"

"I don't believe he ever means earthquakes and cancers," said Mis' Winslow, to her overshoes.

"Prevent 'em, then!" challenged Mis' Bates, triumphantly.

Mis' Winslow looked up. Her eyes were shining as they had shone sometimes when one of her seven-under-fifteen had given its first sign of consciousness of more than self.

"I believe we'll do it some day," she said. "I believe there's more to us than we've got any idea of. I believe there's so much to us that one of us that found out about it and told the rest would get hounded out of town. But even now, I bet there's enough to us to do something every time — something every time, no matter what. And I believe there's something we can do about this little orphand boy's Christmas, if we nip our brains on to it in the right place."

"Oh, dear," said Mis' Moran, "sometimes when I think about Christmas I almost wish we almost hadn't done the way we're going to do."

Mis' Bates stiffened.

"Jane Moran," she said, "do you think it's right to go head over heels in debt to celebrate the birth of our Lord?"

"No," said Mis' Moran, "I don't. But —"

"And you know nobody in Old Trail Town could afford any extravagance this year?"

"Yes," said Mis' Moran, "I do. Still —"

"And if part could and part couldn't, that makes it all the worse, don't it?"

"I know," said Mis' Moran, "I know."

"Well, then," said Mis' Bates triumphantly, "we've done the only way there is to do. Land knows, I wish there was another way. But there ain't."

Mis' Winslow looked up from her overshoes.

"I don't believe there's never 'no other way,'" she said. "There's always another way . . ."

"Not without money," said Mis' Bates.

"Money," Mis' Winslow said, "money. That's like setting up one day of peace on earth, good will to men, and asking admission to it."

"Mis' Winslow," said Mis' Moran, sadly, "what's the use of saying anything? You know as well as I do that Christmas is abused all up and down the land, and made a day of expense and extravagance and folks overspending themselves. And we've stopped all that in Old Trail Town. And now you're trying to make us feel bad."

"I ain't," said Mis' Winslow, "we felt bad about it already, and you know it. I'm glad we've stopped all that. But I wish't we had something to put in its place. I wish't we had."

"What in time are them children doing?" said Mis' Moran, abruptly.

The three women looked. On the side lawn, where a spreading balsam had been left untrimmed to the ground, stood little Emily Moran and Gussie and Bennet and Tab and Pep. And the four boys had their caps in their hands, and Gussie, having untied her own hood, turned to take off little Emily's. The wind, sweeping sharply round the corner of the house, blew their hair wildly and caught at muffler ends. Mis' Bates and Mis' Moran, with one impulse, ran to the side door, and Mis' Winslow followed.

"Emily," said Mis' Moran, "put on your hood this minute."

"Gussie," said Mis' Bates, "put on your cap this instant second. What you got it off for? And little Emily doing as you do — I'm su'prised at you."

The children consulted briefly, then Pep turned to the two women, by now coming down the path, Mis' Bates with her apron over her head, Mis' Moran in her shawl.

"Please," said Pep, "it's a funeral. An' we thought we'd ought to take our caps off till it gets under."

"A funeral," said Mis' Bates. "Who you burying?"

"It's just a rehearsal funeral," Pep explained; "the real one's going to be Christmas."

By now the two women were restoring hood

and stocking cap to the little girls, and it was Mis' Winslow, who had followed, who spoke to Pep.

"Who's dead, Pep?" she asked.

Between the belief of "Who's dead?" and the skepticism of "Who you burying?" the child was swift to distinguish.

"Sandy Claus," he answered readily.

Mis' Winslow stood looking down at him. Pep stepped nearer.

"We're doing it for little Emily," he said confidentially. "She couldn't get it straight about where Sandy Claus would be this Christmas. The rest of us — knew. But Emily's little — so we thought we'd play bury him on her 'count."

Mis' Bates, who had not heard, turned from Gussie.

"Going to do *what* on Christmas?" she exclaimed. "You ain't to do a thing on Christmas. Or ain't you grown up, after all?"

"Well, we thought a Christmas funeral wouldn't hurt," interposed Bennet, defensively. "Can't we even have a funeral for fun on Christmas?" he ended, aggrieved.

"It's Sandy Claus's funeral," observed little Emily putting a curl from her face.

"We're goin' dress up a Sandy Claus, you know," Pep added, *sotto voce*. "It's going to be right after breakfast, Christmas."

"Come on, come ahead, fellows," said Bennet; "I'll be corpse. Keep your lids on. I don't mind. Go ahead, sing."

Already Mis' Winslow was walking back to the house; the other two women overtook her; and from the porch they heard the children begin to sing: —

"*Go bury Saint Nicklis. . . .*"

The rest was lost in the closing of the door.

Back in the sitting room the women stood looking at one another. Mis' Bates was frowning and all Mis' Moran's expressions were on the verge of dissolving; but in Mis' Winslow's face it was as though she had found some new way of consciousness.

"Ladies," Mis' Winslow said, "them children are out there pretending to bury Santa Claus — and so are we. And I bet we can't any of us do it."

In the room, there was a moment of silence in which familiar things seemed to join with their way of saying, "We've been keeping still all the while!" Then Mis' Winslow pushed her hair, regardless of its parting, straight back from her forehead, — a gesture with which she characterized any moment of stress.

"Ladies," she said, "I don't want we should go back on our paper, either. But mebbe there's more to Christmas than it knows about — or than we know about. Mebbe we can do something that won't interfere with the paper we've all signed, and yet that'll be something that is something. Mebbe they's things to use that ain't never been used yet. . . . Oh, I donno. Nor I guess you donno. But let's us find out!"

IX

CHRISTMAS Week came.

Cities by thousands made preparation. Great shops took on vast cargoes of silk and precious things and seemed ready to sail about, distributing gifts to the town, and thought better of it, and let folk come in numbers to them to pay toll for what they took. Banks opened their doors and poured out, now a little trickling stream of pay envelopes, now a torrent of green and gold. Flower stalls drew tribute from a million pots of earth where miracles had been done. Pastry counters, those mock commissariats, delicately masking as servants to necessity, made ready their pretty pretences to nutrition. The woods came moving in — acres of living green, taken in their sleep, their roots left faithful to a tryst with the sap, their tops summoned to bear an hybrid fruitage. From cathedrals rose the voices of children now singing little carols and hymns in praise of the Christ-child, now speaking little verses in praise of the saint, Nicholas, now clamouring for little new possessions. And afar from the fields that lay empty about the clustered roofs of towns came a chorus of voices of the live things, beast and fowl, being offered up in the gorgeous pagan rites of the day.

Hither and yonder in every city the grown townsfolk ran. The most had lists of names, — Grace, Margaret, Laura, Alice, Miriam, John, Philip, Father, Mother, — beautiful names and of rich portent, so that, remembering the time, one would have said that these were entered there with some import of special comradeship, of being face to face, of having realized in little what will some day be true in large. But on looking closer, the lists were found to have quite other connotations: as, Grace, bracelet; Margaret, spangled scarf; Laura, chafing-dish; Philip, smoking set; Father (Memo: Ask mother what she thinks he'd like). And every name, it seemed, stood for some bestowal of new property, mostly of luxuries, and chiefly of luxuries of decoration. And the minds of the buying adults were like lakes played upon by clouds and storm birds and lightning, and, to be sure, many stars — but all in unutterable confusion.

Also from the cargo-laden shops there came other voices in thousands, but these were mostly answers. And when one, understanding Christmas, listened to hear what part in it these behind the counter played, he heard from them no voice of sharing in the theory of peace, or even of truce, but instead: —

"Two a yard and double width. Jewelry

is in the Annex. Did you want three pairs of each? Veils and neckwear three aisles over. Leather, glassware, baskets, ribbons, down the store beyond the notions. Toys and dolls are in the basement — toys and dolls are in the basement. Jewelry is in the Annex. . . ."

So that a great part of the town seemed some strong chorus of invocation to new possessions.

But there were other voices. Whole areas of every town lay, perforce, within the days of Christmas Week — it must have been so, for there is only one calendar to embrace humanity, as there is only one way of birth and breath and death, one source of tears, one functioning for laughter. But to these reaches of the town the calendar was like another thing, for though it was upon them in name, its very presence was withdrawn. In those ill-smelling stairways and lofts there was little to divulge the imminence of anything other than themselves. And wherever some echo of Christmas Week had crept, the wistfulness or the lust was for possession also; but here one could understand its insistence. So here the voices said only, "I wish — I wish," and "I choose this — and this," at windows; or, "If I had back my nickel . . . ." "Don't you go expecting nothink!" And over these went the whirr of machinery, beat of treadles, throb of engines, or the silence of forced idleness, or of the disease of dereliction. It was a time of many pagan observances, as when some were decked in precious stuffs and some were thrown to lions.

To all these in the towns Christmas Week came. And of them all not many stood silent and looked Christmas Week in the face. Yet it is a human experience that none is meant to die without sharing. For the season is the symbol of what happens to folk if they claim it.

Christmas is the time of withdrawal of most

material life. It is the time when nature subtracts the externals, hides from man the phenomena of even her evident processes. Left alone, his thought turns inward and outward — which is to say, it lays hold upon the flowing force so slightly externalized in himself. If he finds in his own being a thousand obstructions, a thousand persons, — dogs, sorcerers, whoremongers, — he will try to escape from them all, back to the externals. But if he finds there a channel which the substance of being is using, he will be no stranger, but a familiar, with himself. Only when the channel has been long cleared, when there has left it all consciousness of striving, of self in any form, only when he finds himself empty, ready, immaculate, will he have the divine adventure. For it is then that in him the spirit of God will have its birth, then that he will first understand his own nature . . . the nature of being.

Then the turn of the year comes in, the year begins to mount. Birth is in it, growth is in it, Spring is in it. Sometime, away back in beginnings, they knew this. They knew that the time of the Winter solstice is in some strange fashion the high moment of the year, as the beginning of new activity in nature and in the gods. They solemnized the return of the fiery sun wheel; they traced in those solstice days the operations on earth of Odin and Berchta. They knew in themselves a thing they could not name. And when the supreme experience took place in Christ, they made the one experience typify the other, and became conscious of the divine nature of this nativity. So, by the illuminati, the prophets, the adepts, the time that followed was yearly set aside — forty days of dwelling within the temple of self, forty days of reverence for being, of consciousness of new birth. Then the emergence, then the apotheosis of expression typifying and typified by Spring — the time when bursting, pressing life almost breaks bounds, when birth and the impulse to birth are in every form of life, without and within. These festivals are not arbitrary in date. They grow out of the universal experience.

Is it not then cause for stupefaction that this time of "divine bestowal" should have become so physical a thing? From the ancient perception, to have slipped into a sense of annual social comradeship and good will and peace was natural and fine — to live in the little what will some day be true in the large. But from this to have plunged down into a time of frantic physical bestowals, of "present trading," of lists of Grace and Margaret and Philip, of teeming shops with hunting and hunted creatures within, of sacrificial trees and beasts, of a sovereign sense of good for me and mine and a

shameless show of Lord and Lady Bountiful
... how can that have come about, how can
the great festival have been so dishonoured?

Not all dishonoured, for within it is its
own vitality which nothing can dishonour.
Through all the curious variations which it receives at our hands, something shines and sings:
self-giving, joy giving, a vast, dim upflicker-
ing on humanity of what this thing really is
that it seeks to observe, this thing that grips
men so that no matter what they are about,
they will drop it at the touch of the gong
and turn to some expression, however crooked
and thwarted, of the real spirit of the time. If
in war, then bayonets are stacked and holly-
wreathed, and candles stuck on each point!
If at sea, some sailor climbs out on the bow-
sprit with a wreath of green. If on the west-
ern plains, a turkey wishbone for target will
make the sport, at fifty paces; if at home, some

great extravagance or some humble gift or some poignant wish will point the day; if at church, then mass and carol; in certain hearts, reverence, — everywhere the time takes hold of folk and receives whatever of greatness or grotesqueness they choose to give it. . . . So, too, the actual and vital experience which it brings to humanity is universal, is offered with cosmic regularity, cannot be escaped. Through all the tumult of the time, Christmas Week and the time that lies near to it is always waiting to claim its own, to take to itself those who will not be deceived, who see in the stupendous yearly pageant only the usual spectacle of humanity trying to say divine things in terms of things physical, because the time for the universal expression is not yet come.

When that time comes . . . when the time of the worship of *things* shall be past; when the tribal sense of holiday shall have given place to the family sense, and that family shall be mankind; when shall never be seen the anomaly of celebrating in a glorification of little family tables — whose crumbs fall to those without — the birth of him who preached brotherhood; and the mockery of observing with wanton spending the birth of him who had not where to lay his head; when the rudiments of divine perception, of self-perception, of social perception, shall have grown to their next estate; when the area of consciousness shall be extended yet farther toward the outermost; when that new knowledge with which the air is charged shall let man begin to know what he is . . . when that time comes, they will look back with utmost wonder at our uncouth gropings to note and honour something whose import we so obscurely discern; but perhaps, too, with wonder that so much of human love and divining should shine for us through the mists we make.

X

Two days before Christmas Ellen Bourne went through the new-fallen snow of their wood lot. Her feet left scuffled tracks clouded about by the brushing of her gown's wet hem and by a dragging corner of shawl. She came to a little evergreen tree, not four feet tall, with low-growing boughs, and she stood looking at it until her husband, who was also following the snow-filled path, overtook her.

"Matthew," she said then, "will you cut me that?"

Matthew Bourne stood with his ax on his shoulder and looked a question in slow preparation to ask one.

"THE CHILDREN BEGAN TO SING 'GO BURY SAINT NICKLIS'"

CHRISTMAS

"I just want it," she said; "I've — took a notion."

He said that she had a good many notions, it seemed to him. But he cut the little tree, with casual ease and no compunctions, and they dragged it to their home, the soft branches patterning the snow and obscuring their footprints.

"It's like real Christmas weather," Ellen said. "They can't stop that coming, anyhow."

In the kitchen Ellen's father sat before the open oven door of the cooking stove, letting the snow melt from his heavy boots.

"Hey," he said, "I was beginning to think you'd forgot about supper. What was in the trap?"

At once Ellen began talking rapidly. "Oh," she said, "we'll have some muffins to-night, father. The kind you like, with —"

"Well, what was in the trap?" the old man

demanded peevishly. "Why don't you answer back? What was, Mat?"

Matthew, drying his ax blade, looked at it with one eye closed.

"Rabbit," he said.

"Where is it?" her father demanded.

"It was a young one — not as big as your fist," Ellen said. "I let it out before he got there. Where's mother?"

"Just because a thing's young, it ain't holy water," the old man complained. "Last time it was a squirrel you let go because it was young — it's like being spendthrift with manna . . . " he went on.

Ellen's mother appeared, gave over to Ellen the supper preparations, contented herself with auxiliary offices of china and butter getting, and talked the while, pleased that she had something to disclose.

"Ben Helders stopped in," she told. "He's

going to the City to-morrow. What do you s'pose after? A boy. He's going to take him to bring up and work on the farm."

"Where's he going to get the boy?" Ellen asked.

Her mother did not know, but Mrs. Helders was going to have a new diagonal and she wanted the number of Ellen's pattern. Ben would stop for it that night.

Evenings their kitchen was a sitting room, and when the supper had been cleared away and the red cotton spread covered the table, Ellen asked her husband to bring in the little tree. She found a cracker box, handily cut a hole with a cooking knife, and set up the little tree by the kitchen window.

"What under the canopy — " said her mother, her voice cracking.

"Oh, something to do in the evening," Ellen answered. "Father's going to pop me some corn to trim it with; aren't you, father? Mother, why don't you get you a good big darning needle and string what he pops?"

"It'll make a lot of litter," said her mother, but she brought the needle, for something to do.

"Hey, king and country," said her father; "I'd ought to have somebody here to shell it for me."

"Who you trimming up a tree for?" her mother demanded; "I thought they wasn't to be any in town this year."

"It ain't Christmas yet," Ellen said only. "I guess it won't do any hurt two days before."

While the two worked, Ellen went to the cupboard drawer, and from behind her pile of kitchen towels she drew out certain things: walnuts, wrapped in shining yeast tinsel and dangling from red yarn; wishbones tied with strips of bright cloth; a tiny box, made like a house, with rudely cut doors and windows; eggshells penciled as faces; a handful of peanut owls; a glass-stoppered bottle; a long necklace of buttonhole twist spools. A certain blue paper soldier doll that she had made was upstairs, but the other things she brought and fastened to the tree.

Her husband smoked and uneasily watched her. He saw somewhat within her plan, but he was not at home there. "If the boy *had* lived and *had* been up-chamber asleep now," he thought once, "it'd be something like, to go trimming up a tree. But *this* way —"

"What you leaving the whole front of the tree bare for?" her mother asked.

"The blue paper soldier goes there. I want it should see the blue paper soldier first thing . . . " Ellen said, and stopped abruptly.

"You talk like you was trimming the tree for somebody," her mother observed, aggrieved.

"Maybe something might look in the window — going by," Ellen said.

"Get in there! Get your heads in there, ye beggars!" said the old man to the popcorn. "I'd ought to have somebody here to pick up them shooting kernels," he complained.

In a little while, with flat-footed stamping, Ben Helders came in. When he had the pattern number, by laborious copying against the wall under the bracket lamp, Matthew said to him : —

"Going to get a boy to work out, are you?"

Helders laughed and shifted.

"He's going to work by and by," he said. "We allow to have him to ourselves a spell first."

"Keep him around the house till Spring?"

"More," said Helders. "You see," he added, "it's like this with us . . . family all gone, all married, and got their own. We figured to get hold of a little shaver and have some comfort with him before he goes to work, for life."

"Adopt him?" said Matthew, curiously.

"That's pretty near it," Helders admitted. "We've got one spoke for at the City Orphand Asylum."

Ellen Bourne turned. "How old?" she asked.

"Around five — six, we figure." Helders said it almost sheepishly.

Ellen stood facing the men, with the white festoons of popcorn in her hands.

"Matthew," she said, "let him bring us one."

Matthew stared. "You mean bring us a boy?" he asked.

"I don't care which — girl or boy. Anything young," Ellen said.

"Good Lord, Ellen," Matthew said, with high eyebrows, "ain't you got your hands full enough now?"

Ellen Bourne lifted her hands slightly and let them fall. "No," she answered.

The older woman looked at her daughter, and now first she was solicitous, as a mother.

"Ellen," she said, "you have, too, got your hands full. You're wore out all the time."

"That's it," Ellen said, "and I'm not wore out with the things I want to do."

"Hey, king and country!" the old man cried, upsetting the popper. "Don't get a child around here underfoot. I'm too old. I deserve grown folks. My head hurts me —"

"Matthew," said Ellen to her husband, "let Helders bring us one. To-morrow — for Christmas, Mat!"

Matthew looked slowly from side to side. It seemed incredible that so large a decision should lie with a man so ineffectual.

"'Seems like we'd ought to think about it a while first," he said weakly.

"Think about it!" said Ellen. "When haven't I thought about it? When have I thought about anything else but him we haven't got any more?"

"Ellen!" the mother mourned, "you don't know what you're taking on yourself —"

"Hush, mother," Ellen said gently; "you don't know what it is. You had me."

She faced Helders. "Will you bring two when you come back to-morrow night?" she said; "and one of them for us?"

Helders looked sidewise at Matthew, who was fumbling at his pipe.

"Wouldn't you want to see it first, now?" Helders temporized. "And a girl or a boy, now?"

"No — I wouldn't want to see it first — I couldn't bear to choose. One healthy — from healthy parents — and either girl or boy," Ellen said, and stopped. "The nicest tree thing I've made is for a boy," she owned. "It's a paper soldier. . . . I made these things for fun," she added to Helders.

For the first time Helders observed the tree. Then he looked in the woman's face. "I'll fetch out a boy for you if you say so," he said.

"Then do," she bade.

When the four were alone again, Mat sat looking at the floor. "Every headlong thing I've ever done I've gone headlong over," he said gloomily.

Ellen took a coin from the clock shelf. "When Ben goes past to-morrow," she merely said, "you'll likely see him. Have him get some little candles for the tree."

"My head hurts me," the old man gave out; "this ain't the place for a great noisy boy."

Ellen put her hand on his shoulder almost maternally.

CHRISTMAS

"See, dear," she said, "then you'd be grandfather."

"Hey?" he said; "not if it was adopted, I wouldn't."

"Why, of course. That would make it ours — and yours. See," she cried, "you've been stringing popcorn for it already, and you didn't know!"

"Be grandfather, would I?" said the old man. "Would I? Hey, king and country! Grandfather again."

Ellen was moving about the kitchen lightly, with that manner, which eager interest brings, of leaving only half footprints.

"Come on, mother," she said, "we must get the popcorn strung for sure, now!"

The mother looked up at the tree. "Seems as if," she said, wrinkling her forehead, "I used to make pink tarleton stockings for your trees and fill 'em with the corn. I donno but I've got a little piece of pink tarleton somewheres in my bottom drawer. . . . "

. . . Next night they had the bracket lamp and the lamp on the shelf and the table hand lamp all burning. The little tree was gay with the white corn and the coloured trifles. The kitchen seemed to be centering in the tree, as if the room had been concerned long enough with the doings of these grown folk and now were looking ahead to see who should come next. It was the high moment of immemorial expectancy, when those who are alive turn the head to see who shall come after.

"What you been making all day, daddy?" Ellen asked, tense at every sound from without.

Her father, neat in his best clothes, blew away a last plume of shaved wood and held out something.

"I just whittled out a kind of a clothespin

man," he explained. "I made one for you, once, and you liked it like everything. Mebbe a boy won't?" he added doubtfully.

"Oh, but a boy will!" Ellen cried, and tied the doll above the blue paper soldier.

"Hadn't they ought to be here pretty soon?" Matthew asked nervously. "Where's mother?"

"She's watching from the front room window," Ellen answered.

Once more Helders came stamping on the kitchen porch, but this time there was a patter of other steps, and Ellen caught open the door before he summoned. Helders stepped into the room, and with him was a little boy.

"This one?" Ellen asked, her eyes alive with her eagerness.

But Helders shook his head.

"Mis' Bourne," he said, "I'm real dead sorry.

They wa'n't but the one. Just the one we'd spoke for."

"*One!*" Ellen said; "you said Orphan Asylum."

"There's only the one," Helders repeated. "The others is little bits of babies, or else spoke for like ours — long ago. It seems they do that way. But I want you should do something: I want you and Matthew should take this one. Mother and I — are older . . . we ain't set store so much . . ."

Ellen shook her head, and made him know, with what words she could find, that it could not be so. Then she knelt and touched at the coat of the child, a small frightened thing, with cap too large for him and one mitten lost. But he looked up brightly, and his eyes stayed on the Christmas tree. Ellen said little things to him, and went to take down for him some trifle from the tree.

"I'm just as much obliged," she said quietly to Helders. "I never thought of there not being enough. We'll wait."

Helders was fumbling for something.

"Here's your candles, I thought you might want them for somethin' else," he said, and turned to Matthew: "And here's your quarter. I didn't get the toy you mentioned. I thought you wouldn't want it, without the little kid."

Matthew looked swiftly at Ellen. He had not told her that he had sent by Helders for a toy. And at that Ellen crossed abruptly to her husband, and she was standing there as they let Helders out, with the little boy.

Ellen's father pounded his knee.

"But how long'll we have to wait? How long'll we have to wait?" he demanded shrilly. "King and country, why didn't somebody ask him that?"

Matthew tore open the door.

"Helders!" he shouted, "how long did they say we'd have to wait?"

"Mebbe only a week or two — mebbe longer," Helders' voice came out of the dark. "They couldn't tell me."

Ellen's mother stood fastening up a fallen tinsel walnut.

"Let's us leave the tree right where it is," she said. "Even with it here, we won't have enough Christmas to hurt anything."

XI

On that morning of the day before Christmas, Mary Chavah woke early, while it was yet dark. With closed eyes she lay, in the grip of a dream that was undissipated by her waking. In the dream she had seen a little town lying in a hollow, lighted and peopled, but without foundation.

"It isn't born yet," they told her, who looked with her, "and the people are not yet born."

"Who is the mother?" she had asked, as if everything must be born of woman.

"You," they had answered.

On which the town had swelled and rounded and swung in a hollow of cloud, globed and shining, like the world.

"You," they had kept on saying.

The sense that she must bear and mother the thing had grasped her with all the sickening force of dream fear. And when the dream slipped into the remembrance of what the day would bring her, the grotesque terror hardly lessened, and she woke to a sense of oppression and coming calamity such as not even her night of decision to take the child had brought to her, a weight as of physical faintness and sickness.

"I feel as if something was going to happen," she said, over and over.

She was wholly ignorant that in that week just passed the word had been liberated and had run round Old Trail Town in the happiest open secrecy: —

". . . coming way from Idaho, with a tag on, Christmas Eve. We thought if everybody could call that night — just run into Mary's, you know, like it was any other night, and take in a little something to eat — no presents, you know . . . oh, of course, no presents! Just supper, in a basket. We'd all have to eat *somewhere*. It won't be any Christmas celebration, of course — oh, no, not with the paper signed and all. But just for us to kind of meet and be there, when he gets off the train from Idaho."

"Just . . . like it was any other night." That was the part that abated suspicion. Indeed, that had been the very theory on which the nonobservance of Christmas had been based: the day was to be treated like any other day. And, obviously, on any other day such a simple plan as this for the welcoming of a little stranger from Idaho would have gone forward as a matter of course. Why deny him this, merely because the night of his arrival chanced to be Christmas Eve? When Christmas was to be treated *exactly* as any other day?

If, in the heart of Mis' Abby Winslow, where the plan had originated, it had originated side by side with the thought that the point of the plan was the incidence of Christmas Eve, she kept her belief secret. The open argument was unassailable, and she contented herself with that. Even Simeon Buck, confronted with it, was silent.

"Goin' back on the paper, are you?" he had at first said, "and hev a celebration?"

"Celebration of what?" Mis' Winslow demanded; "celebration of that little boy getting here all alone, 'way from Idaho. And we'd celebrate that any other night, wouldn't we? Of course we would. Our paper signing don't call for us to give everybody the cold shoulder as I know of, just because it's Christmas or Christmas Eve, either."

"No," Simeon owned, "of course it don't. Of course it don't."

CHRISTMAS

As for Abel Ames, he accepted the proposal with an alacrity which he was put to it to conceal.

"So do," he said heartily, "so do. I guess we can go ahead just like it was a plain day o' the week, can't we?"

"Hetty," he said to his wife, whom that noon he went through the house to the kitchen expressly to tell, "can you bake up a basket of stuff to take over to Mary Chavah's next Tuesday night?"

She looked up from the loaf she was cutting, the habitual wonder of her childish curved lashes accented by her sudden curving of eyebrows.

"Next Tuesday?" she said, "Why, that's Christmas eve!"

Abel explained, saying, "What of that?" and trying to speak indifferently but, in spite of himself, shining through.

"Well, that's kind of nice to do, ain't it?" she answered.

"My, yes," Abel said, emphatically, "It's a thing to do — that's the thing to do."

It was Mis' Mortimer Bates, the nonconformist by nature, in whom doubts came nearest to expression.

"I *don't* know," she said, "it kind of *does* seem like hedging."

"They ain't anybody for it to seem to," Mis' Winslow contended reasonably, "but us. And we understand."

"We was going to do entirely without a Christmas this year. Entirely without," Mis' Bates rehearsed.

"Was we going to do entirely without everyday, week-day, year-in-and-year-out milk of human kindness?" Mis' Winslow demanded. "Well, then, let's us use a little of it, same as we would on a Monday wash day."

No voice was raised in real protest. None who had signed the paper and none who had not done so could take exception to this simple way of hospitality to the little stranger with a tag on. And it was the glory of the little town being a little town that they somehow let it be known that every one was expected to look in at Mary's that night. No one was uninvited. And this was like a part of the midwinter mystery expressing itself unbidden.

Mary alone was not told. She had consistently objected to the Christmas observances for so long that they feared the tyranny of her custom. "She might not let us do it," they said, "but if we all get there, she can't help liking it. She would on any other day . . ."

. . . So she alone in Old Trail Town woke that morning before Christmas with no knowledge of this that was afoot. And yet the day was not like any other day, because she lay there dreading it more.

She had cleared out her little sleeping room, as she had cleared the lower floor. The chamber, with its white-plastered walls, and boards nearly bare, and narrow white bed, had the look of a cell, in the first light struggling through the single snow-framed window. Here, since her childhood she had lain nightly; here she had brought her thought of Adam Blood, and had seen the thought die and had watched with it; here she had lain on the nights after her parents had died; here she had rested, body-sick with fatigue, in the years that she had toiled to keep her home. In all that time there had gone on within her many kinds of death. She had arrived somehow at a dumb feeling that these dyings were gradually uncovering her self from somewhere within; rather, uncovering some self whose existence

CHRISTMAS

she only dimly guessed. "They's two of me," she had thought more often of late "and we don't meet — we don't meet." She lived among her neighbors without hate, without malice; for years she had "meant nothing but love" — and this not negatively. The rebellion against Christmas was against only the falsity of its meaningless observance. The rebellion against taking the child, though somewhat grounded in her distrust of her own fitness, was really the last vestige of a self that had clung to her, in bitterness not toward Adam, but toward Lily. Ever since she had known that the child was coming she had felt a kind of spiritual exhaustion, sharpened by the strange sense of oppression that hung upon her like an illness.

"I feel as if something was going to happen," she kept saying.

In a little while she leaned toward the window at her bed's head, and looked down the hill toward Jenny's. Her heart throbbed when she saw a light there. Of late, when she had waked in the night, she had always looked, but always until now the little house had been wrapped in the darkness. Because of that light, she could not sleep again, and so presently she rose, and in the sharp chill of the room, bathed and dressed, though what had once been her savage satisfaction in braving the cold had long since become mere undramatic ability to endure it without thinking. With Mary, life and all its constructive rites had won what the sacrificial has never been able to achieve — the soul of the casual, of, so to say, second nature, which is last nature, and nature triumphant.

While she was at breakfast Mis' Abby Winslow came in.

"Mercy," Mis' Winslow said, "is it breakfast-early? I've been up hours, frosting the cakes."

"What cakes?" Mary asked idly.

Mis' Winslow flushed dully. "I ain't baked anything much in weeks before," she answered ambiguously, and hurried from the subject.

"The little fellow's coming in on the Local, is he?" she said. "You ain't heard anything different?"

"Nothing different," Mary replied. "Yes, of course he's coming. They left there Saturday, or I'd have heard. The man he's with is going to get home to-night for Christmas with his folks in the City."

"Going down to meet him of course, ain't you," Mis' Winslow pursued easily.

"Why, yes," said Mary.

"Well," Mis' Winslow mounted her preparation, "I was thinking it would be kind of dark for you to bring him in here all alone. Don't you want I should come over and keep up the lights and be here when you get here?"

She watched Mary in open anxiety. If she were to refuse, it would go rather awkwardly. To her delight Mary welcomed with real relief the suggestion.

"I'd be ever so much obliged," she said; "I thought of asking somebody. I'll have a little supper set out for him before I leave."

"Yes, of course," Mis' Winslow said, eyes down. "I'll be over about seven," she added. "If the train's on time, you'll be back here around half past. The children want to go down with you they can be at Mis' Moran's when you go by. You'll walk up from the depot, won't you? You do," she said persuasively; "the little fellow'll be glad to stretch his legs. And it'll give the children a chance to get acquainted."

"I might as well," Mary assented listlessly. "There's no need to hurry home, as I know of, except keeping you waiting."

"Oh, I don't mind," Mis' Winslow told her. "Better come around through town, too. It's some farther, but he'll like the lights. What's the little chap's name?" she asked; "I donno's I've heard you say."

Mary flushed faintly. "Do you know," she said, "I don't know his name. I can't remember that Lily ever told me. They always called him just *Yes*, because he learned to say that first."

"'*Yes*'!" repeated Mis' Winslow, blankly. "Why, it don't sound to me real human."

Later in the day, Mis' Mortimer Bates and Mis' Moran came in to see Mary. Both were hurried and tired, and occasionally one of them lapsed into some mental calculation. "We must remember something for the middle of the table," Mis' Bates observed to Mis' Moran, under cover of Mary's putting wood in the stove. And when Mary related the breaking of the bracket lamp, the two other women telegraphed to each other a glance of memorandum.

"Don't it seem funny to *you* to have Christmas coming on to-morrow and no flurry about it?" Mary asked.

"*No flurry!*" Mis' Bates burst out. "Oh, well," she amended, "of course this Christmas does feel a little funny to all of us. Don't you think so, Mis' Moran?"

"I donno," said Mary, thoughtfully, "but what, when folks stop chasing after Christmas and driving it before them, Christmas may turn around and come to find them."

"Mebbe so," Mis' Moran said with bright eyes, "mebbe so. Oh, Mary," she added, "ain't it nice he's coming?"

Mary looked at them, frowning a little. "It seemed like the thing had to happen," she said; "it'll fit itself in."

Before dark she took a last look about the child's room. The owl paper, the puppy washbasin, the huge calendar with its picture of a stag, the shelves for whatever things of his own he had, all pleased her newly. She had laid on his table her grandfather's Bible with pictures of Asiatic places. Below his mirror hung his father's photograph, that young face, with the unspeakable wistfulness of youth, looking somewhere outside the picture. It made her think of the passionate expectation in the face of the picture that Jenny had brought.

"Young folks in pictures always look like they was setting store by something that ain't true yet," Mary thought. "It makes you kind of feel you have to pitch in and make whatever it is come true, a little. . . ."

It was when Mis' Winslow came back toward seven o'clock that there was news of Jenny. Mary had been twice to her door in the course of the day, and had come away feeling, in her inquiry, strangely outside the moment and alien to its incidence, as if she were somehow less alive than those in Jenny's house.

"Jenny's got a little girl," Mis' Winslow said.

Mary stood staring at her. It seemed impossible. It was like seeing the hands of time move, like becoming momentarily conscious of the swing and rush of the earth, like perceiving the sweep of the stream of stars in which our system moves. . . . She was startled and abashed that the news so seized upon her. Little that had ever happened to herself seemed so poignant, so warmed its place in sensation. While Mis' Winslow's mind marked time on details of time and pounds, as is the way with us immortals when another joins our ranks, Mary was receiving more consciousness. There are times when this gift is laid on swiftly, as with hands, instead of coming when none knows. Rather than with the child whom she was to meet, her thought was with Jenny as she left Mis' Winslow in the doorway and went down the street.

"Expect you back in about half an hour if the train's on time," Mis' Winslow called.

Mary nodded, and turned into the great cathedral aisle that was Old Trail Street, now arched and whitened, spectral in the dark, silver with starlight. . . .

. . . Capella was in the east, high and bright, and as imperative as speech. Mary's way lay north, so that that great sun went beside her, and there was no one else abroad but these two. A coat of ice had polished the walks, so she went by the road, between the long white mounds that lined it. The road, whose curves were absorbed in the dimness, had thus lost its look of activity and lay inert as any frozen waterway. Only a little wind, the star's sparkle, and Mary's step and breath seemed living things — but from the rows of chimneys up and down the Old Trail Road, faint smoke went up, a plume, a wreath, a veil, where the village folk, invisible within quiet roof and wall, lifted common signals; and from here a window and there a window, a light shone out, a point, a ray, a glow, so that one without would almost say, "There's home."

The night before Christmas; and in not one home was there any preparation for tomorrow, Mary thought, unless one or two lawless ones had broken bounds and contrived something, from a little remembrance for somebody to a suet pudding. It was strange, she owned: no trees being trimmed, no churches lighted for practice, and the shops closed as on any other night. Only the post office had light — she went in to look in her box. Affer was there at the telegraph window, and he accosted her.

"Little boy's comin' to-night, is he?" he said, as one of the sponsors for that arrival.

"I'm on my way to the train now," Mary answered, and noted the Christmas notice with its soiled and dog-eared list still hanging on the wall. "It was a good move," she insisted to herself, as she went out into the empty street again.

"You got a merry Christmas without no odds of the paper or me either," Affer called after her; but she did not answer save with her "Thank you, Mr. Affer."

"Why do they all pretend to think it's so fine for me?" she wondered. "To cheer me up, I guess," she thought grimly.

To-night they were all sharing the aloofness from the time, an aloofness which she herself had known for years. All save Jenny. To Jenny's house, in defiance of that dog-eared paper in the post office, Christmas had come.

Not a Christmas of "present trading," not a Christmas of things at all; but *Christmas*. Unto them a child was born.

"Jenny's the only one in this town that's got a real Christmas," thought Mary, on her way to meet her own little guest.

The Simeon Buck North American Dry Goods Exchange was dark, too, and from its cave of window the gray Saint Nicholas looked out, bearing his flag — and he to-night an idle, mummy thing of no significance. The Abel Ames General Merchandise Emporium was closed, but involuntarily Mary stopped before it. In its great plate-glass window a single candle burned. She stood for a moment looking.

"Why, that's what they do, some places, to let the Christ-child in," Mary thought. "I wonder if Abel knows. How funny — for a store!"

CHRISTMAS

Some one whom she did not know passed her and looked too.

"Kind o' nice," said the other.

"Real nice," Mary returned, and went on with a little glow.

Abel's candle, and the arc light shining like cold blue crystal before the dark Town Hall, and the post-office light where the dog-eared list hung and the telegraph key clicked out its pretence at hand touching with all the world, these were the only lights the street showed — save Capella, that went beside her and, as she looked, seemed almost to stand above the town.

At Mis' Moran's house on the other side of the square, the children were waiting for her — Bennet and Gussie and Tab and Pep and little Emily. They ran before Mary in the road, all save little Emily, who walked clasping Mary's hand.

"Aren't you staying up late, Emily?" Mary asked her.

"Yes," assented the child, contentedly.

"Won't you be sleepy?" Mary pursued.

"I was going to stay awake anyhow," she said; "I ain't goin' sleep all night. We said so. We're goin' stay 'wake and see Santa Claus go by."

"Go by?" Mary repeated.

"Yes," the child explained; "you don't think that'll hurt, do you?" she asked anxiously. "And then," she pursued, "if we don't see him, we'll know he's dead everywheres else, too. An' then we're goin' bury him to-morrow morning, up to Gussie's house."

At the station, no one was yet about. The telegraph instrument was clicking there, too, signaling the world; a light showed in the office behind a row of sickly geraniums; the wind came down through the cut and across the tracks and swept the little platform. But the children begging to stay outside, Mary stood in a corner by the telegraph operator's bay window and looked across to the open meadows beyond the tracks and up at the great star. The meadows, sloping to an horizon hill, were even and white, as if an end of sky had been pulled down and spread upon them. Utter peace was there, not the primeval peace that is negation, but a silence that listened.

"'*While shepherds watched their flocks by night, all seated on the ground,...*'" Mary thought and looked along the horizon hill. The time needed an invocation from some one who watched, as many voices, through many centuries, had made invocation on Christmas Eve. For a moment, looking over the lonely white places where no one watched, as no one — save only Jenny — watched in the town, Mary forgot the children. . . .

The shoving and grating of baggage truck wheels recalled her. Just beyond the bay window she saw little Emily lifted to the truck and the four others follow, and the ten heels dangle in air.

"Now!" said Pep. And a chant arose:

"'Twas the night before Christmas when all through the house
Not a creature was stirring, not even a mouse.
The stockings were hung by the chimney with care
In the hope that Saint Nicholas soon would be there. . . ."

Upborne by one, now by another, now by all three voices, the verses went on unto the end. And it was as if not only Tab and Pep and Bennet and Gussie and little Emily were chanting, but all children who had ever counted the days to Christmas and had found Christmas the one

CHRISTMAS 191

piece of magic that is looked on with kindness by a grown-up world. The magic of swimming holes, for example, is largely a forbidden magic; the magic of loud noises, of fast motion, of living things in pockets, of far journeys, of going off alone, of digging caves, of building fires, of high places, of many closed doors, words, mechanisms, foods, ownerships, manners, costumes, companions, and holidays are denied them. But in Christmas their affinity for mystery is recognized, encouraged, gratified, annually provided for. The little group on the baggage truck chanted their watch over a dead body of Christmas, but its magic was there, inviolate. The singsong verses had almost the dignity of lyric expression, of the essence of familiarity with that which is unknown. As if, because humanity had always recognized that the will to Christmas was greater than it knew, these words had somehow been made to catch and reproduce, for generations, some faint spirit of the midwinter mystery.

The 'bus rattled up to the platform and Buff Miles leaped down and blanketed his horses, talking to them as was his wont.

> *"So, holly and mistletoe,*
> *So, holly and mistletoe,*
> *So, holly, and mistletoe,*
> *Over and over and over, oh . . ."*

he was singing as he came round the corner of the station.

"It ain't Christmas yet," he observed defensively to Mary. "It ain't forbid except for Christmas Day, is it?"

He went and bent over the children on the truck.

"Look alive as soon as you can do it," Mary heard him say to them, and wondered.

She stood looking up the track. Across the

still fields, lying empty and ready for some presence, came flashing the point of flame that streamed from the headlight of the train. The light shone out like a signal flashed back to the star standing above the town.

XII

Ten minutes after Mary Chavah had left her house, every window was lighted, a fire was kindled in the parlour, and neighbours came from the dark and fell to work at the baskets they had brought.

It was marvelous what homely cheer arose. The dining-room table, stretched at its fullest length and white-covered, was various with the yellow and red of fruit and salads, the golden brown of cake and rolls, and the mosaic of dishes. The fire roared in the flat-topped stove on whose "wings" covered pans waited, and everywhere was that happy stir and touch and lift, that note of preparation which informs a time as sunshine or music will strike its key.

"My land, the oven — the warming oven.

Mary ain't got one. However will we keep the stuff hot?" Mis' Winslow demanded. "What time is it?"

"We'd ought to had my big coffee-pot. We'd ought to set two going. I donno why I didn't think of it," Mis' Moran grieved.

"Well," said Mis' Mortimer Bates, "when the men get here — if they ever *do* get here — we'll send one of 'em off somewheres for the truck we forgot. What time is it?"

"Here comes a whole cartload of folks," Mis' Moran announced. "I hope and pray they've got the oysters — they'd ought to be popped in the baking oven a minute. What time did you say it is?"

"It's twenty minutes past seven," Mis' Winslow said, pushing her hair straight back, regardless of its part, " and we ain't ready within 'leven hundred miles."

"Well, if they only all get here," Mis' Bates

said, ringing golden and white stuffed eggs on Mary's blue platter; "it's their all being here when she gets here that I want. I ain't worried about the supper — much."

"The road's black with folks," Mis' Moran went on. "I'm so *deadly* afraid I didn't make enough sandwiches. Oh, I donno why it wasn't given me to make more, I'm sure."

"Who's seeing to them in the parlour? Who's getting their baskets out here? Where they finding a place for their wraps? Who's lighting the rest of the lamps? What time is it?" demanded Mis' Winslow, cutting her cakes.

"Oh," said Mis' Bates from a cloud of brown butter about the cooking stove, "I donno whether we've done right. I donno but we've broke our word to the Christmas paper. I donno whether we ain't going to get ourselves criticized for this as never folks was criticized before."

Mis' Moran changed her chair to the draught-less corner back of the cooking stove and offered to stir the savoury saucepan.

"I know it," she said, "I know it. We never planned much in the first start. It grew and it grew like it grew with its own bones. But mebbe there's some won't believe that, one secunt."

Mis' Winslow straightened up from the table and held out a hand with fingers frosting-tipped.

"Well," she said, with a great period, "if we *have* broke our word to the Christmas paper, I'd rather stand up here with my word broke this way than with it kept so good it hurt me. Is it half-past seven yet?"

"I wish Ellen Bourne was here," Mis' Bates observed. "She sent her salad dressing over and lent her silver and her Christmas rose for the table — but come she would not. I wonder if she couldn't come over now if we sent after her, last minute?"

Simeon Buck, appearing a few minutes later at the kitchen door to set a basket inside, was dispatched for Ellen Bourne, the warming oven, and the coffee-pot, collectively. He took with him Abel Ames, who was waiting for him without. And it chanced that they knocked at the Bournes' door just after Ben Helders had driven away with the little boy, so that the men found the family still in the presence of the little tree.

"Hello," said Simeon, aghast, "Christmassing away all by yourselves, I'll be bound, like so many thieves. I rec'lect not seeing your names on the paper."

"No, I didn't sign," Ellen said. "I voted against it that night at the town meeting, but I guess nobody heard me."

"Well," said Simeon, "and so here you've

got a Christmas of your own going forward, neat as a kitten's foot —"

"Ain't you coming over to Mary Chavah's?" Abel broke in with a kind of gentleness. "All of you?"

Ellen smote her hands together.

"I meant to go over later," she said, "and take —" She paused. "I thought we'd all go over later," she said. "I forgot about it. Why, yes, I guess we can go now, can't we? All three of us?"

Abel Ames stood looking at the tree. He half guessed that she might have dressed it for no one who would see it. He looked at Ellen and ventured what he thought.

"Ellen," he said, "if you ain't going to do anything more with that tree to-night, why not take some of the things off, and have Matthew set it on his shoulder, and bring it over to Mary's for the boy that's coming?"

Ellen hesitated. "Would they like it?" she asked. "Would folks?"

Abel smiled. "I'll take the blame," he said, "and you take the tree." And seeing Simeon hesitate, "Now let's stop by for Mis' Moran's coffee-pot," he added. "Hustle up. The Local must be in."

So presently the tree, partly divested of its brightness, was carried through the streets to the other house — in more than the magic which attends the carrying in the open road of a tree, a statue, a cart filled with flowers, — for the tree was like some forbidden thing that still would be expressed.

"*He* might not come till Christmas is 'way past," Ellen thought, following. "She'll leave it standing a few days. We can go down there and look at it — if he comes."

A little way behind them, Simeon and Abel, with the coffee-pot and the warming oven, were

"THEIR WAY LED EAST BETWEEN HIGH BANKS OF SNOW"

hurrying back to Mary's. They went down the deserted street where Abel's candle burned and Simeon's saint stood mute.

"When I was a little shaver," Abel said, "they used to have me stand in the open doorway Christmas Eve, and hold a candle and say a verse. I forget the verse. But I've always liked the candle in doors or windows, like tonight. Look at mine over there now — ain't it like somebody saying something?"

"Well," said Simeon, not to be outdone, "when we come by my window just now, the light hit down on it and I could of swore I see the saint smile."

"Like enough," said Abel, placidly, "like enough. You can't put Christmas out. I see that two weeks ago." He looked back at his own window. "If the little kid that come in the store last Christmas Eve tries to come in again to-night," he said, "he won't find it all pitch dark, anyway. I'd like to know who he was..."

Near the corner that turned down to the Rule Factory, they saw Ebenezer Rule coming toward them on the Old Trail Road. They called to him.

"Hello, Ebenezer," said Abel, "ain't you coming in to Mary Chavah's to-night?"

"I think not," Ebenezer answered.

"Come ahead," encouraged Simeon.

As they met, Abel spoke hesitatingly.

"Ebenezer," he said, "I was just figuring on proposing to Simeon here, that we stop in to your house — I was thinking," he broke off, "how would it be for you and him and me, that sort of stand for the merchandise end of this town, to show up at Mary's house to-night — well, it's the women have done all the work so far — and I was wondering how it would be for us three to get there with some little thing for that little kid that's coming to her — we could find something that wouldn't cost much — it hadn't *ought* to cost much, 'count of our set principles. And take it to him. . . ." Abel ended doubtfully.

Ebenezer simply laughed his curious succession of gutturals.

"Crazy to Christmas after all, ain't you?" he said.

But Simeon wheeled and stared at Abel. For defection in their own camp he had never looked.

"I knew you'd miss it — I knew you'd miss it!" Simeon said excitedly, "cut paper and fancy tassels and —"

"No such thing," said Abel, shortly. "I was thinking of that boy getting here, that's all. And I couldn't see why we shouldn't do our share — which totin' coffee-pots and warming ovens *ain't*, as I see it."

"Well, but my heavens, man!" said Simeon, "it's Christmas! You can't go giving anybody anything, can you?"

"I don't mean give it to him *for* Christmas at all," protested Abel. "I mean give it to him just like you would any other day. We'd likely take him something if it wasn't Christmas? Sort of to show our good will, like the women with the supper? Well, why not take him some little thing even if it is Christmas?"

"Oh, well," said Simeon, "that way. If you make it plain it ain't *for* Christmas — Of course, we ain't to blame for what day his train got in on."

"Sure we ain't," said Abel, confidently.

Ebenezer was moving away.

"We'll call in for you in half an hour or so," Abel's voice followed him. "We'll slip out after the boy gets there. There won't be time before . . . what say, Ebenezer?"

CHRISTMAS 205

"I think not," said Ebenezer; "you don't need me."

"Well — congratulations anyhow!" Abel called.

Ebenezer stopped on the crossing.

"What for?" he asked.

"Man alive," said Abel, "don't you know Bruce has got a little girl?"

"No," said Ebenezer, "I — didn't know. I'm obliged to you."

He turned from them, but instead of crossing the street to go to his house, he faced down the little dark street to the factory. He had walked past Jenny's once that evening, but without being able to force himself to inquire. He knew that Bruce had come a day or two before, but Bruce had sent him no word. Bruce had never sent any word since the conditions of the failure had been made plain to him, when he had resigned his position, refused the salary due him, and left Old Trail Town. Clearly, Ebenezer could make no inquiry under those circumstances, he told himself. They had cut themselves off from him, definitely.

How definitely he was cut off from them was evident as he went down the dark street to the factory. He was strangely quickened, from head to foot, with the news of the birth of Bruce's child. He went down toward the factory simply because that was the place that he knew best, and he wanted to be near it. He walked in the snow of the mid-road, facing the wind, steeped in that sense of keener being which a word may pour in the veins until the body flows with it. The third generation; the next of kin, — that which stirred in him was a satisfaction almost physical that his family was promised its future.

As he went he was unconscious, as he was always unconscious, of the little street. But, perhaps because Abel had mentioned Mary's house, he noted the folk, bound thither, whom he was meeting: Ben Torry, with a basket, and his two boys beside him; August Muir, carrying his little girl and a basket, and his wife following with a basket. Ebenezer spoke to them, and after he had passed them he thought about them for a minute.

"Quite little families," he thought. "I s'pose they get along. . . . I wonder how much Bruce is making a week?"

Nellie Hatch and her lame sister were watching at the lighted window, as if there were something to see.

"Must be kind of dreary work for them — living," he thought, " . . . I s'pose Bruce is pretty pleased . . . pretty pleased."

At the corner, some one spoke to him with a note of pleasure in his voice. It was his bookkeeper, with his wife and two partly grown daughters. Ebenezer thought of his last meeting with his bookkeeper, and remembered the man's smile of perfect comprehension and sympathy, as if they two had something in common.

"Family life does cling to a man," he had said.

That was his wife on his arm, and their two daughters. On that salary of his. . . . Was it possible, it occurred to Ebenezer, that she was saving egg money, earning sewing money, winning prizes for puzzles — as Letty had done?

Outside the factory, the blue arc light threw a thousand shadows on the great bulk of the building, but left naked in light the little office. He stood looking at it, as he so rarely saw it, from part way across the road. Seen so, it took on another aspect, as if it had emerged from some costuming given it by the years. The office was painted brown, and discoloured. He saw it white, with lozenge panes unbroken, flowered curtains at the windows, the light of lamp and wood stove shining out. And as sharply as if it had been painted on the air, he saw some unimportant incident in his life there — a four-wheel carriage drawn up at the door with some Christmas guests just arriving, and himself and Letty and Malcolm in the open doorway. He could not remember who the guests were, or whether he had been glad to see them, and he had no wish in the world to see those guests again. But the simple, casual, homely incident became to him the sign of all that makes up everyday life, the everyday life of folk — *of folks* — from which he had so long been absent.

His eye went down the dark little street where were the houses of the men who were his factory "hands." Just for a breath he saw them as they were, — the chorus to the thing he was thinking about. They were all thinking about it, too. Every one of them knew what he knew. . . . Just for a breath he saw the little street as it was: an entity. Then the sight closed, but through him ran again that sense of keener being, so poignant that now, as his veins flowed with it, something deeper within him almost answered.

He wheeled impatiently from where he stood. He wanted to do something. At the end of the street he could see them crossing under the light, on their way to Mary Chavah's. Abel and Simeon might stop for him . . . but how could he go there, among the folk whom he had virtually denied their Christmas? What would they have to say to him? Yet what they should say would, after all, matter nothing to him . . . and perhaps he would hear them say something about Bruce and Jenny. Still, he had nothing to take there, as Abel had suggested. What had he that a boy would want to have? Unless . . .

He thought for a moment. Then he crossed the street to what had been his house. He went in, seeing again the hallway and stair, red-carpeted, and the door opened into the lamplit room beyond. He found and lighted an end of candle that he knew, and made his way up the stair. There he set the candle down and lowered the ladder that led to the loft.

In the loft, a gust of wind from the skylight blew out the flame of his little wick. In the darkness, the broken panes above his head looked down on him like a face, and that face the sky, thousand-eyed. He mounted a box, pushed up the frame, and put out his head. The sky lay near. The little town showed, heaped roofs and lifting smoke, and here and there a light. Sparkling in their midst was the light before the Town Hall, like an eye guarding something and answering to the light before his factory and to the other light before the station, where the world went by. High over all, climbing the east, came Capella, and seemed to be standing above the village.

As he looked, the need to express what he felt beset Ebenezer.

"Quite a little town," he thought, "quite a little town."

He closed the glass, and groped in the darkness to where the roof, sloping sharply, met the door. There he touched an edge of something that swayed, and he laid hold of and drew out that for which he had come: Malcolm's hobbyhorse.

Downstairs in the hall he set it on the floor, examined it, rocked it with one finger. The horse returned to its ancient office as if it were irrevocably ordained to service. Ebenezer, his head on one side, stood for some time regarding it. Then he slipped something in its worn saddle-pocket. Last, he lifted and settled the thing under his arm.

"I donno but I might as well walk around by Mary Chavah's house," he thought. "I needn't stay long. . . ."

At Mary Chavah's house the two big parlours, the hall, the stairs, the dining room, even the tiny bedroom with the owl wall paper, were filled with folk come to welcome the little boy. And on the parlour table, set so that he should see it when first he entered, blazed Ellen Bourne's little tree. The coffee was hot on the stove, good things were ready on the table, and the air was electric with expectation, with the excitement of being together, with the imminent surprise to Mary, and with curiosity about the little stranger from Idaho.

"What'll we all say when he first comes in?" somebody asked.

"Might say 'Merry Christmas,'" two or three suggested.

"Mercy, no!" replied shocked voices, "not to Mary Chavah, especially."

But however they should say it, the time was quick with cheer.

At quarter to eight the gate clicked. The word passed from one to another, and by the time a step sounded on the porch the rooms were still, save for the whispers, and a voice or two that kept unconsciously on in some remote corner. But instead of the door opening to admit Mary and her little boy, a hesitating knock sounded.

Those nearest to the door questioned one another with startled looks, and one of them threw the door open. On the threshold stood Affer, the telegraph operator, who thrust in a very dirty hand and a yellow envelope.

"We don't deliver nights," he said, "but I thought she'd ought to have this one. I'm going home to wash up, and then I'll be back," he added, and left them staring at one another around the little lighted tree.

XIII

BEFORE they could go out to find Mary, as a dozen would have done, she was at the threshold, alone. She seemed to understand without wonder why they were there, and with perfect naturalness she turned to them to share her trouble.

"He hasn't come," she said simply.

Her face was quite white, and because they usually saw her with a scarf or shawl over her head, she looked almost strange to them, for she wore a hat. Also she had on an unfamiliar soft-coloured wrap that had been her mother's and was kept in tissues. She had dressed carefully to go to meet the child. "I might as well dress up a little," she had thought, "and I guess he'll like colours best."

CHRISTMAS

Almost before she spoke they put in her hands the telegram. They were pressing toward her, dreading, speechless, trying to hear what should be read. She stepped nearer to the light of the candles on the little tree, read, and reread in the stillness. When she looked up her face was so illumined that she was strange to them once more.

"Oh," she said, "it's his train. It was late for the Local. They've put him on the Express, and it'll drop him at the draw."

The tense air crumpled into breathings, and a soft clamour filled the rooms as they told one another, and came to tell her how glad they were. She pulled herself together and tried to slip into her natural manner.

"It did give me a turn," she confessed; "I thought he'd been — he'd got . . ."

She went into the dining room, still without great wonder that they were all there; but when she saw the women in white aprons, and the table arrayed, and on it Ellen Bourne's Christmas rose blooming, she broke into a little laugh.

"Oh," she said, "you done this a-purpose for *him*."

"I hope, Mary, you won't mind," Mis' Mortimer Bates said formally, "it being Christmas, so. We'd have done just the same on any other day."

"Oh," Mary said, "*mind!*"

They hardly knew her, she moved among them so flushed and laughing and conformable, praising, admiring, thanking them.

"Honestly, Mary," said Mis' Moran, finally, "we'll have you so you can't tell Christmas from any other day — it'll be so nice!"

The Express would be due at the "draw" at eight-thirty — eight-thirty-three, Affer told her when he came back, "washed up." Mary watched the clock. She had not milked or fed the cows before she went, because she had thought that *he* would like to watch the milking, and it would be something for him to do on that first evening. So, when she could, she took her shawl and slipped out to the shed for the pails and her lantern, and went alone to the stable.

Mary opened the door, and her lantern made a golden room of light within the borderless shadow. The hay smell from the loft and the mangers, the even breathing of the cows, the quiet safety of the place, met her. She hung her lantern in its accustomed place, and went about her task.

Her mind turned back to the time that had elapsed since the Local came in at the Old Trail Town station. She had stood there, with the children about her, hardly breathing while the two Trail Town men and a solitary traveling man had alighted. There had been no one else. In terror lest the child should be carried past the station, she had questioned the conductor, begged him to go in and look again, parleyed with him until he had swung his lantern. Then she had turned away with the children, utterly unable to formulate anything. There was no other train to stop at Old Trail Town that night. It must mean disaster . . . indefinable disaster that had somehow engulfed him and had not pointed the way that he had gone. She recalled, now, that she had refused Buff Miles's invitation to ride, but had suffered him to take the children. Then she had set out to walk home.

On that walk home she had unlived her plans. Obscure speculations, stirring in her fear, at first tormented her, and then gave place to the conclusion that John had changed his mind, had seen perhaps that he could not

CHRISTMAS

after all let the child go so far, had found some one else to take him; and that the morrow would bring a letter to tell her so. In any case, she was not to have him. The conclusion swept her with the vigour of certainty. But instead of the relief for which she would have looked, that certainty gave her nothing but desolation. Until the moment when the expectation seemed to die she had not divined how it had grown into her days, as subtly as the growth of little cell and little cell. And now the weight upon her, instead of lifting, soaring in the possibility of the return of her old freedom, lay the more heavily, and her sense of oppression became abysmal. . . . "Something is going to happen," she had kept saying. "Something *has* happened. . . ."

So she had got on toward her own door. There the swift relief was like an upbearing into another air, charged with more intimate largess for life. Now Mary sat in the stable in a sense of happy reality that clothed all her feeling — rather, in a sense of superreality, which she did not know how to accept. . . . So, slowly singing in her as she sat at her task, came that which had waited until she should open the way. . . .

In the stable there was that fusion of shadow and light in which captive spaces reveal all their mystery. Little areas of brightness, of functioning; then dimness, then the deep. Brightness in which surfaces of worn floor, slivered wall, dusty glass, showed values more specific than those of colour. Dimness in which gray rafters with wavering edges, rough posts each with an accessory of shadow, an old harness in grotesque loops, ceased to be background and assumed rôles. The background itself, modified by many an unshadowed promontory, was accented in caverns of manger and

CHRISTMAS

roof. The place revealed mystery and beauty in the casual business of saying what had to be said.

Mary filled her arms with hay, and turned to the manger. The raw smell of the clover smote her, and it was as sweet as Spring re-promised. She stood for a moment with the hay in her arms, her breath coming swiftly. . . .

Down on the marsh, not half an hour away, he was coming to her, to be with her, as she had grown used to imagining him. She had thought that he was not coming, and he was almost here. . . . She knew now that she was glad of this, no matter what it brought her; glad, as she had never known how to be glad of anything before. He was coming — there was a thrill in the words every time that she thought them. Already she was welcoming him in her heart, already he was here, already he was born into her life. . . .

. . . With a soft, fierce rush of feeling not her own, it seemed to her that her point of perception was somehow drawn inward, as if she no longer saw from the old places, as if something in her that was not used to looking, looked. In the seat where her will had been was no will. But somewhere in there, beyond all conflict, she felt *herself* to be. Beyond a thousand mists, volitions, little seekings for comfort, rebellions at toil, the cryings of personality for its physical own, she stood at last, herself within herself. And that which, through the slow process of her life and of life and being immeasurably before her, had been seeking its expression, building up its own vehicle of incarnation, quite suddenly and simply flowered. It was as if the weight and the striving within her had been the pangs of some birth. She stood, as light of heart as a little child, filled with peace and tender exaltation.

These filled her on the road which she took to meet him — and took alone, for she would have no one go with her. ("What's come over Mary?" they asked one another in the kitchen. "She acts like she was somebody else and herself too.") The night lay about her as any other winter night, white and black, — a clean white world on which men set a pattern of highway and shelter, a clean dark sky on which a story is written in stars; and between — no mystery, but only growth. Out toward the drawbridge the road was not well broken. She went, stumbling in the ruts and hardly conscious of them. And Mary thought —

"Something in me is glad.

"It's as if something in me knew how to be glad more than I ever knew how alone.

"For I'm nothing but me, here in Old Trail

Town, and yet it's as if Something had come, secret, on purpose to make me know why to be glad.

"It's something in the world bigger than I know about.

"It's in me, and I guess it was in folks before me, and it will be in folks always.

"It isn't just for Ebenezer Rule and the City.

"It's for everybody, here in Old Trail Town as much as anywhere.

"It's for folks that's hungry for it, and it's for folks that ain't.

"It's always been in the world and it always will be in the world, and some day we'll know what to do."

But this was hardly in her feeling, or even in her thought; it lay within her thanksgiving that the child was coming; and he only a little way down there across the marsh.

... It seemed quite credible and even fitting that the mighty, rushing, lighted Express, which seldom stopped at Old Trail Town, should that night come thundering across the marsh, and slow down at the drawbridge for her sake and the little boy's. Several coaches' length from where she stood she saw a lantern shine where they were lifting him down. She ran ankle deep through the thinly crusted snow.

"*That's* it!" said the conductor. "All the way from Idaho!" and swung his lantern from the step. "Merry Christmas!" he called back.

The little thing clasping Mary's hand suddenly leaped up and down beside her.

"Merry Christmas! Merry Christmas! Merry Christmas!" he shouted with all his might.

Mary Chavah stood silent, and as the train drew away held out her hand, still in silence, for the boy to take.

As the noise of the train lessened, he looked up.

"Are you her?" he asked soberly.

"Yes," she cried joyously, "I'm her!"

Their way led east between high banks of snow. At the end of the road was the village, looking like something lying on the great white plate of the meadows and being offered to one who needed it. At the far end of the road which was Old Trail Road, hung the blue arc light of the Town Hall, center to the constellation of the home lights and the shop lights and the street lights. There, in her house, were her neighbours, gathered to do no violence to that Christmas paper of theirs, since there was to be no "present trading," no "money spending."

Nevertheless, they had drawn together by common consent, and it was Christmas Eve. She knew it now: There is no arbitrary shutting out of that for which Christmas stands. As its spirit was in the village, so its spirit is in the world — denied indeed, put upon, crowned with mockery, dragged in the dirt, bearing alien burdens, but through it all immaculate, waiting for men to cross the threshold at which it never ceases to beckon to a common heritage: Home of the world, with a thousand towers shining with uncounted lights, lying very near — above the village, at the end of the Old Trail Road, upon the earth at the end of a yet unbeaten path — where men face the sovereign fact of humanhood.

... But all this lay within Mary's dumb thanksgiving that the child was running at her side. And the vision that she saw streamed down from Capella, of the brightness of an hundred of our suns, the star that stood in the east above the village where she lived.

Lanterns glowed through the roadside shrubbery, little kindly lights, like answers; and at a bend in the road voices burst about them, and Buff Miles and the children, Gussie and Bennet and Tab and Pep and little Emily, ran, singing, and closed about Mary and the child, and went on with them, slipping into the "church choir Christmas carols," and more, that Buff had been fain to teach them. The music filled the quiet night, rose, in the children's voices, like an invocation to all time.

> *"One for the way it all begun,*
> *Two for the way it all has run,*
> *What three'll be for I do forget,*
> *But what will be has not been yet.*

*So holly and mistletoe,
So holly and mistletoe,
So holly and mistletoe
Over and over and over, oh!"*

Between songs the children whispered together for a minute.

"What's the new little boy's name?" asked Tab.

Nobody knew. That would be something to find out.

"Well," Tab said, "to-morrow morning, right after breakfast, I'm going to bring Theophilus Thistledown down and *lend* him to him."

"Ain't we going to bury Sandy Claus right after breakfast?" demanded Gussie.

And all the children, even little Emily, answered:

"No, let's not."

They all went on together and entered

Mary's gate. Those within,— hearing the singing, had opened the door, and they brought them through that deep arch of warmth and light. Afterward, no one could remember whether or not the greeting had been "Merry Christmas," but there could have been no mistaking what everybody meant.

XIV

At his gate in the street wall lined with snow-bowed lilacs and mulberries, Ebenezer Rule waited in the dark for his two friends to come back. He had found Kate Kerr in his kitchen methodically making a jar of Christmas cookies. ("You've got to eat, if it is Christmas," she had defended herself in a whisper.) And to her stupefaction he had dispatched her to Mary Chavah's with her entire Christmas baking in a basket.

"I don't believe they've got near enough for all the folks I see going," he explained it.

While he went within doors he had left the hobbyhorse in the snow, close to the wall; and he came back there to wait. The street had emptied. By now every one had gone to

Mary Chavah's. Once he caught the gleam of lanterns down the road and heard children's voices singing. For some time he heard the singing, and after it had stopped he fancied that he heard it. Startled, he looked up into the wide night lying serene above the town, and not yet become vexed by the town's shadows and interrupted by their lights. It was as if the singing came from up there. But the night kept its way of looking steadily beyond him.

. . . It came to Ebenezer that the night had not always been so unconscious of his presence. The one long ago, for example, when he had slept beneath this wall and dreamed that he had a kingdom; those other nights, when he had wandered abroad with his star glass. Then the night used to be something else. It had seemed to meet him, to admit him. Now he knew, and for a long time had known, that when he was abroad in the night he was there, so to say, without its permission. As for men, he could not tell when relation with them had changed, when he had begun to think of them as among the externals; but he knew that now he ran along the surface of them and let them go. He never met them as *Others*, as belonging to countless equations of which he was one term, and they playing that wonderful, near rôle of *Other*. Thus he had got along, as if his own individuation were the only one that had ever occurred and as if all the mass of mankind — and the Night and the Day — were undifferentiated from some substance all inimical.

Then this vast egoism had heard itself expressed in the mention of Bruce's baby — the third generation. But by the great sorcery wherewith Nature has protected herself, this mammoth sense of self, when it extends unto the next generations, becomes a keeper of the race. Ebenezer had been touched, relaxed, disintegrated. Here was an interest outside himself which was yet no external. Vast, level reaches lay about that fact, and all long unexplored. But these were peopled. He saw them peopled. . . .

. . . As in the cheer and stir within the house where that night were gathered his townsfolk, his neighbours, his "hands." He had thought that their way of meeting him, if he chose to go among them, would matter nothing. Abruptly now he saw that it would matter more than he could bear. They were in there at Mary's, the rooms full of little families, getting along as best they could, taking pride in their children, looking ahead, looking ahead — *and they would not know that he understood*. He could not have defined offhand what it was that he understood. But it had, it seemed, something to do with Letty's account book and Bruce's baby. . . .

Gradually he let himself face what it was that he was wanting to do. And when he faced that, he left the hobbyhorse where it was under the wall and went into the street.

He took his place among the externals of the Winter night, himself unconscious of them. The night, with all its content, a thing of explicable fellowships, lay waiting patiently for those of its children who knew its face. In the dark and under the snow the very elements of earth and life were obscured, as in some clear wash correcting too strong values. He moved along the village, and now his dominant consciousness was the same consciousness in which that little village lived. But he knew it only as the impulse that urged him on toward Jenny's house. If he went to Jenny's, if he signified so that he wished not to be cut off from her and

Bruce and the baby, if he asked Bruce to come back to the business, these meant a lifetime of modification to the boy's ideals for that business, and modification to the lives of the "hands" back there in Mary Chavah's house — and to something else. . . .

"What else?" he asked himself.

Mechanically he looked up and saw the heavens crowded with bright watchers. In that high field one star, brighter than the others, hung over the little town. He found himself trying to see the stars as they had looked to him years ago, when they and the night had seemed to mean something else. . . .

"What else?" he asked himself.

The time did not seem momentous. It was only very quiet. Nothing new was there, nothing different. It had always been so. The night lay in a sovereign consciousness of being more than just itself. "Do you think that you are all just you and nothing else?" it was seen to be compassionately asking.

"What else?" Ebenezer asked himself.

He did not face this yet. But in that hour which seemed pure essence, with no attenuating sound or touch, he kept on up the hill toward Jenny's house.

Mary Chavah left ajar the door from the child's room to the room where, in the dark, the tree stood. He had wanted the door to be ajar "so the things I think about can go back and forth," he had explained.

In the dining room she wrapped herself in the gray shawl and threw up the two windows. New air swept in, cleansing, replacing, prevailing. Her guests had left her early, as is the way in Old Trail Town. Then she had had her first moments with the child alone. He had done the things that she had not thought of his doing but had inevitably recognized: Had delayed his bed-going, had magnified and repeated the offices of his journey, had shown her the contents of his pockets, had repeatedly mentioned by their first names his playmates in Idaho and shown surprise when she asked him who they were. Mary stood now by the window conscious of a wonderful thing: That it seemed as if he had been there always.

In the clean inrush of the air she was aware of a faint fragrance, coming to her once and again. She looked down at her garden, lying wrapped in white and veiled with black, like some secret being. Three elements were slowly fashioning it, while the fourth, a soft fire within her, answered them. The fragrance made it seem as if the turn of the year were very near, as if its prophecy, evident once in the October violets in her garden, were come again. But when she moved, she knew that the fra-

"THE THREE MEN STEPPED INTO THE LAMPLIGHT"

grance came from within the room, from Ellen Bourne's Christmas rose, blossoming on the table. . . . Above, her eye fell on the picture that Jenny had brought to her on that day when she had all but emptied the house, as if in readiness. Almost she understood now the passionate expectation in that face, not unlike the expectation of those who in her dream had kept saying "You."

There was a movement in her garden and on the walk footsteps. The three men stepped into the rectangle of lamplight — Abel Ames and Simeon, who had left the party a little before the others and, hurrying back with the gifts that they planned, had met Ebenezer at his gate, getting home from Jenny's house. In Abel's arms was something globed, like a little world; in Simeon's, the tall, gray-gowned Saint Nicholas taken from the Exchange window, the lettered sign absent, but the little flag still in his hand; and Ebenezer was carrying the hobbyhorse. If at him the other two had wondered somewhat, they had said nothing, in that fashion of treating the essential which is as peculiar to certain simple, robust souls as to other kinds of great souls.

"Has the boy gone to bed?" Abel asked without preface.

"Yes," Mary answered, "he has. I'm sorry."

"Never mind," Simeon whispered, "you can give him these in the morning."

Mary, her shawl half hiding her face, stooped to take what the three lifted.

"They ain't presents, you know," Abel assured her positively. "They're just — well, just to let him know."

Mary set the strange assortment on the floor of the dining room — the things that were to be nothing in themselves, only just "to let him know."

"Thank you for him," she said gently. "And thank you for me," she added.

Ebenezer fumbled for a moment at his beaver hat, and took it off. Then the other two did so to their firm-fixed caps. And with an impulse that came from no one could tell whom, the three spoke — the first time hesitatingly, the next time together and confidently.

"Merry Christmas. Merry Christmas," they said.

Mary Chavah lifted her hand.

"Merry Christmas!" she cried.

THE following pages contain advertisements of Macmillan books by the same author, and new fiction

THE OTHER BOOKS OF MISS GALE

Mothers to Men

Decorated cloth, 12mo, $1.50 net; by mail, $1.62

The author is singularly successful in detaching herself from all the wear and tear of modern life and has produced a book filled with sweetness, beautiful in ideas, charming in characterizations, highly contemplative, and evidencing a philosophy of life all her own.

"One of the most widely read of our writers of short fiction." — *The Bookman.*

Friendship Village

Cloth, 12mo, $1.50

"As charming as an April day, all showers and sunshine, and sometimes both together, so that the delighted reader hardly knows whether laughter or tears are fittest." — *The New York Times.*

The Loves of Pelleas and Etarre

Cloth, 12mo, $1.50

"It contains the sort of message that seems to set the world right for even the most depressed, and can be depended upon to sweeten every moment spent over it." — *San Francisco Chronicle.*

Friendship Village Love Stories

Decorated cloth, gilt top, 12mo, $1.50

Miss Gale's pleasant and highly individual outlook upon life has never been revealed to better advantage than in these charming stories of the heart affairs of the young people of Friendship Village.

THE MACMILLAN COMPANY

Publishers   64–66 Fifth Avenue   **New York**

NEW MACMILLAN FICTION

A Man's World
By ALBERT EDWARDS
Cloth, 12mo, $1.25 net; postpaid, $1.36

"A striking book that should attract wide attention." — *New York Tribune.*

"There never has been a book like 'A Man's World.' . . . A novelist of skill and power. . . . His greatest gift is his power of creating the illusion of reality. . . . Vividness and conviction unite in the wonderful portrait of Nina. . . . There never has been such a character in American fiction before. . . . Nina will be one of the famous twentieth century heroines." *Brooklyn Eagle.*

"It is a great book, full of the real things of life. . . . Zola might have written such a book had he lived in New York and not in Paris. Yet, it is doubtful if he could have told a better tale in a better way, for Nina and Ann are just as true to life as Nana and Ninon." — *Chicago Record-Herald.*

"The book is far from ordinary and its philosophy is extraordinary." — *New York Times Book Review.*

"A new type of human document — written in all sincerity and honesty." — *New York Herald.*

My Love and I
By MARTIN REDFIELD
Cloth, 12mo, $1.35 net; postpaid, $1.47

Even the publishers do not know who the author of this remarkable book is. Its pages tell with powerful reality the struggle of a heart against the subtler problems of love and a solution not usually found in fiction. It is not an ordinary love story; it is, on the contrary, the intimate confession of a man's life.

THE MACMILLAN COMPANY
Publishers   **64-66 Fifth Avenue**   **New York**

NEW MACMILLAN FICTION — *Continued*

The Rich Mrs. Burgoyne

By KATHLEEN NORRIS
Author of "Mother"

Decorated cloth, 12mo, illustrated, $1.25 net; postpaid, $1.38

When it is rumored about in Santa Paloma that Mrs. Burgoyne, a widow and heiress to many millions, has bought an old-fashioned and somewhat run-down estate and intends to make her home in the little California town, food for gossip at all the bridge clubs is furnished for more than one meeting. To live well in Santa Paloma involves heavy expenditures for all sorts of social functions and many a family feels the strain which, however, they would not admit for worlds. The society clique think that everything will be run on even a more gorgeous scale with Mrs. Burgoyne's millions in the game, but they reckon without the possessor of these millions, as the successive events of the story show in a highly entertaining fashion.

London Lavender

By E. V. LUCAS

Decorated cloth, 12mo, $1.35 net; postpaid, $1.47

We meet again several of the fine characters with whom Mr. Lucas has already made us acquainted in his other novels as well as others equally interesting and entertaining. The intimate sketches of various phases of London life — visits to the Derby, Zoo, the National Gallery — are delightfully chronicled and woven into a novel that is a most charming entertainment.

THE MACMILLAN COMPANY
Publishers   **64-66 Fifth Avenue**   **New York**

NEW MACMILLAN FICTION — *Continued*

The Drifting Diamond

By LINCOLN COLCORD

With Frontispiece in Colors by ANTON FISCHER

Decorated cloth, 12mo, $1.25 net

The strange effects which the possession of a gem of marvelous beauty and great value has upon several sharply differentiated characters is the thread with which this dramatic tale of events is woven. The combination of the mystical, the imaginative and the realistic makes very unusual reading. The diamond has the power of making its owner love it not for what it means in money, but for itself; it also has in it a lurking devil which portends evil happenings. The series of incidents which these qualities in the gem bring about, taken with the love story, which runs through it all, comprise a novel which holds the reader's attention from the very first adventure to the final outcome.

A NEW NOVEL

By JAMES LANE ALLEN

The Heroine in Bronze

Decorated cloth, 12mo, $1.35 net

In "The Heroine in Bronze" Mr. Allen has written with exquisite felicity of thought and expression a novel that is unique and powerful. The story of a young man, — a writer, — the women he loves, and the great novel he writes, is the design threading a background which reveals Mr. Allen's profound understanding of life and his high spirituality. "The Heroine in Bronze" is the most vital contribution to American literature in recent years.

THE MACMILLAN COMPANY

Publishers   64-66 Fifth Avenue   **New York**

A BEAUTIFUL EDITION OF A BEAUTIFUL STORY

THE CHRISTMAS EDITION OF KATHLEEN NORRIS'S

Mother

Decorated cloth, 12mo, illustrations, $1.25; by mail, $1.36

"A little book that can be finished in an hour, but the sweet thoughts will remain in the mind long after the book has been set aside. . . . Before I had covered ten pages I realized that I had something worth its weight in gold. What theme could be more interesting to the ordinary reader than 'Mother,' especially when it is a panegyric on maternal devotion? The author was fortunate in her selection and still happier in her treatment of it, for if there is anything that appeals, it is a true loyal discussion of mother and mother-love. In modern fiction we have too little of the chastening and purifying presence of real motherhood. Few books have the power of recalling worthy thoughts with the force and with the good effect possessed by this little book." — *Catholic Columbian.*

A NEW EDITION OF A MASTERPIECE

THE CHRISTMAS EDITION OF JACK LONDON'S

The Call of the Wild

Decorated cloth, 12mo, profusely illustrated in color,
$1.50 net; by mail, $1.63

To all readers of Jack London and particularly to those who love his masterpiece, this new edition of "The Call of the Wild" will mean much. Some of the previous issues of this great book were thought to be beautiful, but none of them seems so now in comparison with the latest one, the make-up of which is distinguished by a number of features. In the first place there are many full-page plates reproduced in color from paintings done by Mr. Bransom. More than this, the first two pages of each chapter are printed in colors and decorated with head pieces and drawings, while every other two pages carry black and white half tones in the text, also the work of Mr. Bransom.

THE MACMILLAN COMPANY

Publishers   64-66 Fifth Avenue   New York